The Salmiya Collection

Stories of the Life and Times of Modern Kuwait ≈

Craig Loomis

SYRACUSE UNIVERSITY PRESS

First Edition 2013
13 14 15 16 17 18 6 5 4 3 2 1

Many stories in this collection were originally published in *bazaar,* a monthly Kuwaiti magazine, from 2004 to 2012. They are reprinted here with permission.

This is a work of fiction. Names, characters, places, dialogues, and incidents either are the product of the author's imagination or are used fictitiously. Any resemblance to actual persons living or dead, business establishments, events, or locales is entirely coincidental.

∞ The paper used in this publication meets the minimum requirements of the American National Standard for Information Sciences—Permanence of Paper for Printed Library Materials, ANSI Z39.48-1992.

For a listing of books published and distributed by Syracuse University Press, visit our website at SyracuseUniversityPress.syr.edu.

ISBN: 978-0-8156-1014-4

Library of Congress Cataloging-in-Publication Data

Loomis, Craig.
[Short stories Selections]
The Salmiya collection : stories of the life and times of modern Kuwait / Craig Loomis. — First edition.
pages cm
ISBN 978-0-8156-1014-4 (pbk. : alk. paper) 1. Kuwait—Social life and customs—21st century—Fiction. 2. Kuwait—Social conditions—21st century—Fiction. I. Title.
PS3612.O562S35 2013
813'.6—dc23 2013001281

Manufactured in the United States of America

For Rebecca, Persis, and Saleah

Craig Loomis is currently an associate professor of English at the American University of Kuwait. Much of his short fiction has been published in literary journals and magazines worldwide, from the *Iowa Review, Colorado Review, Quarterly West,* and *Louisville Review,* in the USA, to the *Prague Revue* in the Czech Republic.

Contents

Acknowledgments

I would especially like to thank the staff of *bazaar* magazine (Kuwait) for being so supportive and accommodating of my work over the years.

Introduction

Kuwait is a small country, about the size of New Jersey, wedged neatly in between Iraq and Saudi Arabia. For the longest time it was a dusty, sleepy township, minding its own business; like a lot of small countries—as well as a handful of big ones—Kuwait was not important to the world stage. If given a map, people could not put their finger on it. *One of those new overnight countries in Africa? Something just south of Russia?* However, all that changed in 1938 when oil was discovered in the Kuwaiti desert. Fifty-two years later, on 2 August 1990, when Saddam Hussein's Iraq decided that invading Kuwait was a good idea, the small country once again made headlines. Within six months, the international community removed Iraq from Kuwait and the tiny country was once again free, with oil, to mind its own business. Ever since then, Kuwait has grown bigger, brighter, faster—and everything in between.

The Salmiya Collection

The Reprimand

It is the sort of knock that could have been mistaken for something else: someone dropping a shoe, children thumping against the wall, the creaking of an old, tired ceiling. But then it comes again.

"Sorry to bother you, sir."

"Yes, quite all right. What can I do for you, Siera?"

Glancing over his shoulder, once, twice, until, "It's Nasser, Mrs. Nasser, sir."

"Who?"

"The Nassers, the woman over there," pointing over his head, into the wall, window, and beyond, "and her family, a very old family I think. They have been here for years, you know. Before I came, way before I came. In fact, they say the Nasser family owns all there," sweeping his arm that way, "and there," another sweeping the other way, towards a swath of buildings, park, and one or two elementary schools. "You have seen their cars, I think. Two long brown Chrysler New Yorkers, and maybe more, you see. Maybe much more."

Nodding, and still holding the door wide open for Siera, who has yet to come in, to cross the threshold. "Rather well off, are they?"

"Yes I think so."

"Well," rubbing his chest and then shuffling back, away from the door, "would you like to come in?"

"No, no," holding up one hand.

"But you didn't come here to tell me this," smiling. "The wealthy people of Kuwait." Although it is not much of a joke, he laughs like it is, and Siera, the *haris*, the building manager, decides to laugh with him.

"No I don't come to tell you about that, but you see it's Ramadan, and Mrs. Nasser and her family, all families who are Muslims, are, of course, fasting."

"Yes, I know all this."

"Of course, well," looking over his shoulder a third, longer time, until . . .

"Are we looking for someone, Siera?"

"No, no, it's just that as you say, it's Ramadan, and Mrs. Nasser is concerned, this much I can tell you. Maybe even worried."

"Really, whatever for?"

"Well, sir, it's about you. She tells me she is concerned about you." All finished looking over his shoulder, he starts to fold and refold his arms across his chest.

"Me?" fingers to his chest.

"Yes sir, you see it's Ramadan and . . ."

"Yes, I know. We've already established that."

"Well, Mrs. Nasser had a birthday the other day, a big party. I'm sure you heard the people, many people from all over; and someone gave her a very fine present, very fine, and she is using this present now, every day, she tells me."

Both of them standing in the doorway, the elevator moaning up and down behind them.

"Yes, well, this present of hers is binoculars, sir. Someone, maybe an uncle, or aunt, who's to say, but someone gave them to her for sure and she likes her new binoculars very much. Shiny new German made."

"Yes, binoculars."

He had learned that it does no good to rush them, to hurry them; after ten—no eleven—years, he understands their pace, their way of circling, of moving closer then back, closer, back, until finally . . .

"Yes, and she was exercising her binoculars today, this morning in fact. Looking at the birds, the cars. She likes to look at so many things with her German-made binoculars. Many things."

"Exercising her binoculars?"

"Yes."

They stop to hear the traffic, the sirens of the city. Between elevator groans a big silence fills and refills the hallway. They are almost there now, the finish line growing big, bigger.

"And?"

"And, sir, she was exercising those binoculars of hers this way, like I said, towards you, your apartment."

"She did?" He turns to look back into his apartment, as if to remind himself what it looks like. "But, there's nothing to see. See, nothing."

"Yes, this way," motioning toward the window, "and she saw you sir."

"She did?"

"Yes, this is what she told me."

"Siera, you mean she saw me earlier, by the car, outside. That's what you mean."

"No, sir, now, today, twenty, fifteen minutes ago, maybe less. She saw you through the curtains."

Again turning to see for a second time, and yes, the curtains are closed.

"Maybe there," his finger pointing to one of those small places in the middle of the window that no curtain can get to, where the smallest crack of light and glass peeks through.

"There?"

"Maybe there she saw you."

"Well that's not so bad, is it? What's to see?"

"Yes, well." All done folding and refolding, his arms at his sides soldier-like. Finally, " . . . Well, she tells me she saw you eating, chewing something like bread, maybe a sandwich, she said. That's what she said, 'Chewing something like a sandwich.'"

Now it is his turn to fold, refold.

"Yes sir, eating during Ramadan, during fasting; sir, she is concerned about you."

Taking a deep breath and looking back at his window, the tiny triangle of uncurtained glass, then back at Siera, the sweat bright across his cheeks. "She's complaining about me eating during Ramadan?"

For the first time Siera smiles. "Yes, that's it sir. Exactly."

"Exercising her binoculars?"

"Yes sir, exactly. Thank you, sir."

The Ballad of Reedah

"There he is," she whispers, nudging Reedah with her shoulder.

"Where?"

"There, the tall one with the Manchester United shirt. See?"

As they slow, Reedah turns to take a good hard look.

"Don't stop," says her mother, "Keep walking. Don't stare like that, what's wrong with you. Glance, glance, don't stop."

"Are you sure that's him? He's the one?"

It is then that the mother stops, grabbing Reedah's sleeve extra tight. "Of course I'm sure. I've seen the photo, his mother showed me, and that's him. I told you, it's all planned. Now go, introduce yourself. Why do you always do this?"

Reedah has not taken off her sunglasses since she entered the mall, and now, as they start walking again, she shakes her head. "I don't think so, Mama. No, this will not work."

Getting a bigger, better grip on Reedah's sleeve, she turns to face her daughter, whispering louder, "We have been through this before, many times before, and enough is enough."

"Yes, yes, but it's not right."

"What? What is this not right? What's not to like?"

"This," and Reedah uses both hands to churn the air in front of her, "This . . . These coffee shop chats, these measuring sessions, these . . ."

But her mother's hand will not let go, will not give up that easily. "This what? You haven't even spoken to him yet, and look, look he has such a nice smile. See that? And the teeth, the whitest teeth. That's something. Right? See that? Reedah, speak to the man, give him a chance, you never give them a chance. Do it for me, for your father. For Baba."

Because Reedah is twenty-eight years old, soon to be twenty-nine, her mother has been worrying for the last four years. In fact, she tells Reedah that the whole family is worried as well, the uncles and aunts and cousins in Cairo are worried, asking quietly but firmly, "What's wrong with Reedah? Twenty-eight, going on twenty-nine and still nothing like a boyfriend in sight. Something not right here, something all wrong. Now, I have a friend whose son. . . ."

In the end, with Mr. Manchester United looking down at his cellphone and now smoking a cigarette and now going back to his cellphone, he sits down, and Reedah, taking a deep breath, removes her sunglasses and walks toward him. Meanwhile, her mother moves to a nearby coffee shop, watching all, ordering a hot tea that she will never drink.

Reedah introduces herself, shaking his hand, and together they sit. Reedah has strong, rough hands but only her mother worries about this. Her mother tells her to use lotion, creams. "Rub long and hard, every night. At twenty-eight your hands should be soft and supple, everybody knows this." For the next thirty minutes they talk the talk of such coffee shop meetings: of jobs, education, salaries, families. He tells two jokes about Arabs living in London. Finally, their talk all used up, he leans over and, looking down at the tabletop to brush off something that isn't there, says, "You know, my parents are religious people, always have been. Firm believers."

"That's good," she answers, turning ever so slightly to spy her mother.

"Yes, and because they are religious people, they, and even me, would want my wife to understand the importance of covering, of wearing the *hijab*. My parents, and me too, we think this is a good idea. Don't you agree?"

Reedah uses both hands to push her hair out of her eyes, long black hair that on windy days swirls around her neck and face like a warm friendly mist. And so as he waits and smiles his white teeth, she returns his smile and says nothing.

Later that night, with dinner over and the TV showing some Turkish soap opera that no one is watching, Reedah's mother clears her throat, looks at the TV that no one is watching and turns to Reedah, saying, "What are you waiting for? They are all nice boys with potential; they come from respectable families. *Sah?* They have gone to the best universities, and some will become doctors, engineers, important businessmen. Their futures are bright. *Sah?* What are you waiting for? What do you want?"

Reedah, having heard this before, has learned that anger is no longer useful, and answers her mother by looking straight into the TV that nobody is watching, saying, "I don't know."

"What?"

"I said I don't know."

"How can you not know at twenty-eight, almost twenty-nine? What's to know? It's marriage time, yes?" By now, tears are streaming down her cheeks, slipping into the corners of her mouth. As Reedah waits, hands folded, suddenly, like a kind of magic, her mother is holding a tissue, wiping her face clean, and now blowing her nose, her face still wet and red. "Reedah, time is running out. It already may be too late."

Meanwhile, on the couch, newspaper in hand, sits Reedah's father, who, on hearing this last part, slowly closes the paper across his lap. He watches, listens, and says nothing. Reedah glances at the newspaper, then at him, and he smiles and winks.

She gets up, announcing, "I'm going to my room now, Mama."

"To your room, always to your room. What is wrong with you, Reedah?"

To this her father clicks his tongue.

"What is wrong with you? I wonder, we all wonder. What?"

"Good night, Mama."

Once in her room, locking the door behind her, Reedah is more tired than angry; these talks almost always exhaust her. And as she lies on her bed, staring up into the creamy white of the ceiling, she thinks, just for a moment, that she understands what is going on, why this hunt for a husband is not working, will never work, and yes, she knows that it has nothing to do with family names or college degrees or having soft hands, that it has nothing to do with straight white teeth. It has nothing to do with any of that, but she doesn't know the name for what's left.

The Untimely Death of Number 431

More of a poof than an explosion. More of a sandy spray wrapped in a thud than the loud blazing stuff of death. That, and they all were looking that direction when it happened, as if someone had tapped them on the shoulder, saying, "Stop everything and watch this, right over there. Ready?" A plume of sand and dirt rising high and orange. That's when they saw her, in the very center of the poof, one of her back legs pinwheeling a meaty red high over her head. And when everything stopped, she was over there, her leg over here, and everything else was sprinkled in a new dirty-brown desert.

His best and oldest camel, Number 431, had been doing what she knows best: minding her own business, chewing, staring off into the desert, chewing some more—always some more—when she wrong-footed onto one of those forgotten Iraqi landmines that the government had promised was no more. There had been a clicking just before the poof, a clicking in the middle of the desert that should have warned someone of something about to go all wrong.

His *imamah* flapping flag-like, and now unspooling as he ran, Mohammed screeched, "What have you done?"

"Nothing."

Looking at the two boys, one his son, he went on, "How can this be? What did you do?"

"Nothing."

"Yes something."

"Nothing."

"How did you do that?"

"It wasn't me," both hands at his chest to show him me.

"We've grazed this land west of the highway for what, five, six years, maybe more? And now this?"

Meanwhile, camel 431 had become her own mound, more graybrown than red, trying to turn her head with brown eyes bulging to see who was coming and what was what. As he rushed toward her, he pushed his son aside, the boy stumbling, falling. Yusuf, the other, the un-son, had seen this before, the same sort of explosion with sheep, once even some teenager's brand new jeep somersaulting, all smoke and spinning tires. So, he hurried to hold up his hands, to stop him, pleading, "No, no, stay there."

"What?" His unwound *imamah* catching up with him, "Why?"

"Stay, stay. It's a bomb, a weapon, a mine, Yes, a mine."

"What mine?"

"The mines of war."

Still on the ground, his son had stopped to listen as well. They all stopped to hear, to see what the landscape of mines looked like.

"Yes, the war, the invasion, I've heard the stories."

The son done listening now, got up, brushing off the dirt and rockgrit, making certain his cellphone was still there.

Number 431, having heard all, hadn't stopped looking, her mound grown darker as a cloud moved in, her neck growing tired and heavy until her head finally gave up, pitching into the earth.

Of course, like so many of them, in the beginning, Number 431 had been terrible: all spitting and kicking and bawling, the line of tiny copper bells that looped her neck crashing around her; but then later, after a few beatings and much talking to, she grew calm, obedient, even dog-like. And for the last four years she had been the best of them all.

Tiptoeing, looking extra hard and long at the ground now, and when he finally got to her, she hadn't stopped chewing, her eyes showing more white than eyeball, blinking fast and hard to push the sand away; and although he rubbed her neck and tried his best to reassure her that everything will be all right, "Just you wait and see. Don't move. Stay still, . . . still," she was having none of it and one last time struggled to get up. In the meantime, a tiny river of blood streamed from the place of her once leg, seeping quickly into the sands, having no chance to pool or puddle.

Mohammed couldn't believe his bad luck. First, Noura, his wife of twenty-six years and mother of one son and three daughters, giving up to what the doctor had said was something like cancer, only worse; and then no more than a week after that, his favorite uncle hit and killed by some young motorcyclist one night in Salmiya. The boy insisting that it wasn't his fault because the bright headlights had blinded him, because he didn't see the red light, and because 'My cousin is a policeman, and . . .'

With the boys standing side by side, Mohammed rose, looking first at the distant highway with its insect-like cars and trucks, then back to Number 431 and then off to the East and the brown smudge of Jahra, and then, in the end, at his other five camels that had never stopped drifting deeper into the desert. As he walked by his son, he pushed him full in the chest, back into the sand.

"What's that for?"

Not even bothering to stop but walking after his other camels, turning his head to half speak to the desert, half to his son, saying, "She was the best of them all. The very best. And now this. They said they had cleared the bombs, the mines. The Americans, the

British, Kuwait, somebody said it was done and safe, and now this, . . . this."

With his final "this" still lingering in the air, something hard and tinkling bounced in front of him, and then to his right, and then a little farther to his right. He reached down and picked up two tiny copper bells. He held them close to his face, and yes, they were hers. Another one of her bells thudded over there, among the rocks, and there behind the boys. He looked up into the sky and could only think, *Impossible.* It was then, as he threw the copper bells down and turned to march after his other camels that for the second time that morning the desert clicked.

The Older Brother

"So this English 100 class, this . . . what? . . ." spinning his hands like he knows something about twirling, maybe even some magic tricks, " . . . developmental writing class cannot be right for Saba. She needs something more challenging, something bigger, better, you understand. Her teachers have called her superior. Since elementary school, level one, they have called her superior."

Before he can continue, the cellphone that he had so neatly placed on the table, to his right, next to the swirl of prayer beads, twinkles, jingles, and the best he can do is grab it, turn sidewise and talk into the curtains. Together we wait for him. She twice runs her fingers around the rim of her *hijab,* searching for anything that might be loose, out, dangling. Meanwhile, not once has he allowed the caller a chance to respond, to say yes, no, or maybe; he is, in fact, one long line of gruff Arabic. She turns to look into the hallway, where two girls are talking, giggling. Finally he snaps the phone shut, says, "Excuse," straightens his *dishdasha,* hands on tabletop. He has a fine moustache and a finer watch. He on my left, she on my right.

They came in together, he leading the way. His handshake was weak, almost unimportant, but I have learned that that doesn't mean anything, not the way it used to. He was already in mid-sit before I could finish saying, "Please, have a seat."

I turn to ask her about her superior writing.

"She has always earned good marks, you see."

"Tell me about some of the things you have written: essays, stories, maybe some poetry? Perhaps you have brought some samples for me to look at?"

"Yes, Saba's written all of these things, and more. She's the best, I tell you, number one." Thumbs up like an astronaut.

All the while, except to perfect her *hijab,* she hasn't taken her fingers away from her lips, not once, only nodding. He picks up his prayer beads, sits back in the chair and sighs like this is work, this talking to professors about his sister's writing, and he needs a break, some kind of second wind. The giggling girls have moved on, farther down the hallway, and in their place is a boy, books at his chest, waiting his turn. That's when I hold up the paper that has her placement score, that says she should be in the developmental writing class. "Saba, your test score is not very good. It says you should take this English 100. You know, students take placement tests for a reason; the purpose of such tests is not to punish but to help, to. . . ." They are old arguments, ones that I have used often during the last two days of registration. Arguments I no longer believe in.

Surprisingly, she looks directly at me, her fingers leaning to the right, and says, "Yes, I see." But then I make the mistake of glancing his way, and quickly, as if he feels there is a tide of sorts and it is turning against him, he cups his beads in both hands and leans forward, saying, "Yes, she understands what placement tests are. We all understand, but I tell you she is ready for this other course, this credit course, this more advanced 101 class."

I look to see if she agrees, but there are only fingers at the lips, and blinking.

"You see, I've studied in the States, MBA Maryland, you know the Fighting Terps?" This last part bringing his biggest, best smile. "So I have seen this good writing many times—maybe hundreds of times. I have done it myself. I know what you are looking for; we all know, and this one has it. Saba, . . ." motioning toward her, as if she is more than just a tabletop away, "came to visit me once—remember?" She nods yes she remembers. "My first year at College Park—remember?" Nodding that she still remembers. "Anyway, let's come back to this . . ." placing his hand in the center of the table and dragging it slowly toward him, "this writing test, this placement test." Taking a deep breath, "Professor, sometimes these tests don't tell the truth, you see. Sometimes, in their own way they lie, or only tell part of what is true. This is the case with this one, Saba. Your tests don't tell the truth. She does not need this non-credit English 100. She is ready for the other, the credit, the bigger class."

"Are you?"

"Yes," he says.

"Are you?"

"Yes, Saba, please tell the professor. Please explain to him how this English 100 . . ." looking quickly to his left, then right, as if the English 100 class was here a moment ago, but now, when he wasn't looking, disappeared, " . . . is not for you."

Her fingers curl away from her lips, for just a moment, and when they do I can see that her teeth are almost perfect: white, straight across. In a whisper she says, "Yes, what my brother tells you is true. All true."

"See. There it is. See, just like I said." Smiling first at his hands, then at me, as if *There, it's done, settled. Nice talking with you.*

In the end, the boy with textbooks at his chest hasn't stopped waiting, and I turn to her and recommend that she take the developmental class, English 100.

"Recommend." He snatches at the word. Although it sounds like a question, it really isn't. "Recommend. Is this the word I'm hearing? Recommend?"

“Yes, recommend.”

“Fine,” pushing back, rising, holding out his hand for one final shake. “Fine, recommend. You hear that Saba, recommend.”

She nods and hurries to stand, and now out of nowhere she too has a cellphone that needs talking to.

Even though he is standing, moving toward the door, he goes on and I nod like he is talking wisdom, but I have heard it all before, if not from older brothers, then from well-read mothers, fathers who know important people, uncles who own construction companies, car rentals, shopping centers.

Once Upon a Time and Not So Far Away

"What's the matter with him?"

"I don't know. What did you do to him?"

"I didn't do anything," he said. "It's time to go to the park. He knows that. I didn't do anything."

She walked over and stood beside him, and together they looked down at the dog.

He was an old black dog whose teeth were no longer any good. They fed him soft, expensive meats—the sort that needed only one or two good chews before going down. And while she almost always mixed in an egg with the meat, her husband never did. In fact, Peter Spears had never even considered it.

"What's the matter with him?"

The black dog was under the desk and wouldn't come out. She leaned down and looked in. His big shaggy head looked happy to see her. His tail drummed against the floor.

"What's the matter, boy?"

When Peter Spears knelt to join them, he was met with a hollow growling, something like a moan. The dog's tail stopped.

"What's the matter with you?"

From the shallow cave under the desk, he watched Peter Spears. His small watery eyes refused to blink; his teeth, ancient and bone-worn, peeked out. The old dog watching Peter Spears closely. From deep within the city came the long, thin talk of a siren, while on the wall, above their heads ticked the big clock.

"He doesn't seem to like you today," she said, standing up. She pushed back her hair as if it had been in her face, in her eyes, but it hadn't.

"What's the matter with him?"

"I don't know," she sighed.

"Maybe he's sick."

The dog was very still. Only his small watery eyes moved.

Again she pushed back her hair.

"Worms," said Peter Spears slowly scratching his chest. "Maybe he's got worms."

"Worms?" She folded her arms and looked down. One black paw stuck out. "Worms?"

"Sure. It happens all the time. Worms."

And the paw disappeared under the desk.

"Maybe," sighing again. "We'll see."

His tail thumped against the floor. Peter Spears nodded, glancing one last time at his wife as he walked away. "What's the matter with him?"

She thought about kneeling to look one last time but then, at the last moment, decided against it.

"Strange. He likes the park." The big golden clock on the wall ticking. "He likes the park, doesn't he?" But when she turned for an answer he was gone. Pushing back her hair. "Worms?"

On the bedroom chair was Peter Spears's coat. He slipped it on. Although the country was too warm for a coat, he didn't care because that's where he kept his papers, in the coat pocket. They rarely asked for papers anymore, but for the last two years, ever since the Andrewses, he never went anywhere without them—just in case. Besides, by the looks of things it was beginning to go bad again. Peter Spears had been in the country long enough to know when things were getting ready to go bad again. It was a dirty gray coat, and he buttoned it all the way up to his throat.

She was waiting for him at the door. "You're sure you didn't give him a swat or anything? He doesn't like being swatted, you know. Nobody likes to be swatted. You really shouldn't swat him like that."

"But I didn't swat him." He held out his hands to show her. "I didn't do anything."

She nodded, and then reached out to feel his coat pocket. There was the soft crush of paper. He looked down at her short brown hair; she was staring into his coat, into the buttons. Peter Spears secretly counted ten ticks of the clock.

"All right, I'm off."

"Peter?"

The faint cry of somebody's rooster, and the old dog thumped in agreement.

"Peter," now looking into his face. "Peter, be careful."

He knew it had been something. All morning long it had been something, but he hadn't thought of that. "What do you mean?"

She saw how he had buttoned his coat all the way up, and when she reached to touch the top button she couldn't think of what to do next. "I don't know. You know how they can be sometimes. You know how they are at times like this." She fixed his collar. "Remember the Andrewses?" A big black nose edging out from under the desk.

"Listen, I've got two hours. I'll be back long before curfew. You know that." Peter Spears reached out and touched the soft whorl of her ear. She closed her eyes. "What's wrong with everybody? First the dog, now you. I'm just going to the park. I've done it a hundred times, two hundred times."

She opened her eyes and pressed his hand hard against her forehead. "You're right," she shrugged, and took a step back.

From the door to the street was ten giant steps. He had taken five of the ten when . . .

"Peter."

Standing in the doorway like that made her look slim, even young. It reminded him of a scene from some old movie.

"Peter." She let her arms fall to her sides and stood very straight. "Peter, be careful."

He waved good-bye, finished counting his steps and then turned right. She pushed back her hair and watched him walk past the trees and disappear around the corner.

When a warm breeze met Peter Spears at the corner, he unbuttoned the top button. The trees along the street were large and cool. He didn't know what kind of trees they were—just large and cool. He walked down a well-worn path. Every now and again chunks of jagged concrete peeked up along the way, but the path always slithered neatly around them. Although Peter Spears walked with his hands in his pockets, he really didn't have to. The warm breeze hissed through the treetops. For some reason—and he'd given it some thought—it all seemed perfectly correct: the hard brown path, the small wind through the leaves, the white prehistoric concrete. In a small Middle Eastern way it was perfectly right. That's all, perfectly correct. The park wasn't far.

When Peter Spears finally decided to look up, he saw a woman and a child coming down the path toward him. The woman was fat and wearing a black *abaya*. The little girl wore a lavender dress. But there was something wrong with the girl; she moved as if she needed crutches, or maybe had some sort of crazy sickness that had nothing to do with crutches. She clung to the fat woman's arm, and together they laughed. They disappeared behind a large fang of concrete, and when they emerged he saw what the little girl was all about: she was on roller-skates. Taking his hands out of his pockets, Peter Spears stepped into the long grass, letting them pass. They went by just that way: large black on unsteady purple. And every time the little girl slipped, she'd grab hold of a huge black sleeve, laughing long and loud. Even after they turned the corner he could hear their laughter over the hissing trees.

At the end of the street was a thin, almost useless tree, and it was here where the old dog would make him stop. He liked to sniff and walk around it—that's all he ever did. And so, when Peter Spears came to the tree, he stopped. Behind it and to the right was a big calico cat, followed by a bigger black cat. Ears flat against their heads, their backs cameled, they taunted one another with hollow catty moans. Their tails twitched electric. They saw him but didn't care. Finally the pathway grew weak and unimportant, and Peter Spears turned to walk in the street. It wouldn't be much longer now.

It was a straight walk from the street to the park, but where there should have been a path there was only gravel—a long barren field of gravel. Off to the right, in front of a broken half-wall, squatted three children cooking handfuls of gravel in rusty pans. He watched them and tried to listen. They stirred the gravel in their pans, stopping every now and again to add another stone, another scoop of pebbles to their gravel fire. As he started across the lake of gravel, the smallest, brownest of them stood up, straddled one of the pans and peed into it. The others were quiet, but nodded approvingly. It took Peter Spears a long time to crunch across to the park because he kept stopping, looking back.

Tall, black clouds were beginning to roll in over the city from the east. The wind grew rougher, cooler. He could feel it at his ankles, at his neck. Patches of dust jittered into the trees. He pulled up his collar.

It wasn't until the park that he saw soldiers. Like always they were all shiny black boots, tangles of leather strapping, golden insignias, pistols riding their hips, the silver wink of rifles. They stood under the trees, at the edge of the pond. If it hadn't been for their guns, the tight graygreen of their uniforms, they could have been just about anybody: cab drivers, football fans. . . . But the rifles—muzzles skyward—and the fact that they never seemed to laugh, not even a smile, gave them away.

The approaching storm marbled in the twilight. Peter Spears hurried to one of the benches. He crossed his legs, smoothed back his hair and watched the sky. At first it was pretty: the way the setting sun burned through the clouds, shooting purple back into the city. But then, even as he watched, its prettiness slowly began to drain into the horizon, and in its place loomed the blacks and grays of a stormy night. The wind tugged at his hair. At the end of the bench, between the cracks, he could see where it had once been green. Small scabs of green paint still clung to the wood.

And so the soldiers were standing under the trees, and then he saw two old people down by the pond. The old people were talking. He couldn't hear them but he could see them gesturing, glancing. The man had a cane, and he leaned on it like he really needed it; the woman, smaller, almost childlike, leaned against him as if she needed a cane too. One cane for two old people. They gestured, shuffled, and stopped, gestured, shuffled and stopped . . .

The old black dog was a good walker. In the house he was weak, even feeble, but once out the door and it was one continuous taut leash until they reach the thin tree. "What's the matter with him?" He looked down at his shoes. They were smooth and toe-scarred. She had wanted to throw them away but he liked them. After all these years they were just starting to be friendly shoes. Ever since that time he broke his foot in a high school football game, shoes had been unkind to him. Peter Spears shuffled his feet, his shoes. He wished the dog had come with him.

The next time he looked, the old people had moved away from the pond. They teetered along the hedges. Two soldiers walked by. They were smoking cigarettes and looking intently at a scrap of paper one of them held. The taller, sharp-jawed one glanced at him but then almost immediately went back to the paper. Leaning back now, he looked left, at the knoll with its cluster of wheat-colored rocks. For some reason one of the very best things about the park was the wheat-colored rocks. When the two soldiers stepped off the grass and onto the gravel, a soft metallic clicking began. One of them tossed his cigarette, the other tugged at his rifle strap. The clicking stopped. A tiny pinpoint of siren wailed from the city center. It was then, with the soldiers crunching over the gravel, that Peter Spears thought about the Andrewses.

Franklin Andrews had been two things: big and likable. There should have been more; everybody who had known him wanted there to be more, but there wasn't. On the other hand his wife, Peggy, a tiny blonde from some important East Coast family, had been all the things that Franklin probably should have been: loud, arrogant, brash. To remember Peggy Andrews was to recall a person who had spent a great deal of time and energy being angry. Her eyes would flash, her eyebrows jack-knife. There had always been new and exciting Peggy Andrews anger stories to tell. Finally there had been their son Jack. But because Jack had been just like his dad, only bigger, he was easily forgettable. So, there was the three of them. That was two years ago.

That was the autumn when the small country had decided to go through one of its bad times. The nights were filled with a steady zigzag of deep city sirens, of flashing red and blue lights. There was gunfire and the glow of fires. A car bomb had shattered all the windows in two banks, and somebody's daughter lost both legs. Strange gray ambulances cruised the streets after dark. The soldiers had gotten new uniforms, new weapons, and they spent all day walking up and down the streets. Even the half-naked children played soldier in the streets, down the dirty back-alleys, in front of their broken homes.

It was during this time two years ago that the small country said everyone needed to carry papers. Peter Spears was even issued papers saying that his old black dog was in fact his old black dog. And so it went.

However, since Peggy Andrews didn't think people should have to carry papers, she, of course, didn't—wouldn't. 'Nobody should have to carry three sheets of paper to prove who they are. Nobody.'

Autumn was almost over when the Andrewses disappeared. Their apartment, food, clothing, goldfish, everything, stayed behind, but the three of them vanished.

When news of their disappearance surfaced, everybody who knew them thought it was terrible. It was a shame Peggy refused to carry her papers. Because of Peggy's important East Coast family, a thorough investigation was conducted. After six months of investigating, an official report went back to the East Coast saying that Peggy and family had—"for the time being"—disappeared, but the authorities would—"you can rest assured"—continue to look for them.

It was during the heavy heat of springtime that another family moved into the Andrewses' apartment. They fixed up the walls and planted yellow flowers along the balcony.

Lightning veined across the sky. Peter Spears looked up to watch some children near the pond, an assortment of tiny blueandgray figures throwing rocks into the water. Someone was driving across the gravel. An army jeep going too fast, the dust billowing up like steam.

Lightning jumped, and a long line of purple trickled out of the sunset. The storm was growing. But then, like a magic, the wind died away, and where there should have been noise, there was nothing. The clouds churned silently. The air grew still. Two more rocks plunked into the pond, and even the children stopped to look. The soft bench wood slipped easily under his fingernails. Click. Click. He turned to see. But there was only the long gray of gravel, the trees, the ghostly outline of the city. . . . Like having the bedside telephone ring in the middle of the night, there was that jumping in his throat, throbbing in his ears. There was a clicking—he had heard it! But where there should have been something, there was nothing.

When the children began throwing rocks again, Peter Spears stood up. But as he turned to leave, he noticed something off to the side, a shadowy fidgeting. Someone had stepped out from under the trees and was moving toward him. A crack of thunder. He unbuttoned his coat and got ready to show his papers. He took one step toward the bench, leaning forward to get a better look. It was a woman—an old woman.

She hobbled toward him. Holding on to the bench with one hand, Peter Spears snapped off a scab of dead paint. The old woman walked up to the bench, stopped, lifted her head. Her face was brown and worn; deep, fleshy furrows swirled over her face. Not knowing what else to do, he offered her his papers. She looked up at his face and then down at his outstretched papers. A great white flicker injected a moment's daylight over the park. She stood there blinking, as if she were trying to remember something. His hands were wet and sticky and he tried wiping them on his pants.

"What do you want?" The sound of his own voice startled him. She sighed a deep sigh, and with the back of her withered hand wiped her chin. Her lips moved.

"What?"

The storm was everywhere now. Raindrops hitting him on the cheek. She moved her lips but there were no words. Then, as if it had all been some terrible mistake, she sighed another long sigh, and shuffled away. Peter Spears, pushing the rain away from his eyes, watched her disappear into the mist.

Now that she was gone, he could see there had been nothing to it. He had been at the bench and she had simply walked to where he was. For one confusing moment their lines had bumped into one another, tangled—that's all. Nothing to it, just one of those things.

The pond was dark and quiet. The children were gone. He wondered where they could have disappeared to so quickly. It was late—almost too late. He would have to hurry.

Two steps onto the gravel and Peter Spears began to run. He hadn't meant to run, a fast walk would have been enough, but when his feet crunched on the gravel, his legs bolted—spooked like some wide-eyed animal—and it was all he could do to follow. He locked his teeth and ran into the wind.

He made it as far as the trees on his street before staggering, falling. He clung to one of the tree trunks for help, but when he groped for a better hold, the leathery bark broke off in his hands. It felt strangely warm, warmer than he remembered trees ever being. The old football injury throbbed like a second heart. Peter Spears gulped but his body didn't seem to care if it got enough air or not. The nausea came in large waves, licking his throat. And just when he should have vomited, he didn't, couldn't, and it all went spiraling back down. He slumped over the wet tree roots, wondering why his legs had spooked like that. His arms slipped from the tree. His legs twitched as if they wanted to go on without him.

The wind was back, bullying its way through the treetops. The rain charging down in a black slant. His clothes sucked wet and shiny. It was then that he saw shadows shifting under the trees. Shapeless grays rolled, fluttered and then easily, almost magically, righted themselves. Peter Spears stopped, stared. Something was there. He strained to listen but his body was making too much noise. His chest heaved. The air seemed to dribble into his lungs. But yes, something was there—under the trees. He could hear a quiet, half-talk, followed by a faint underwater murmuring, as if people were praying. He crouched. A soft stormlight moved across the sky, and he heard . . .

"But I love you. Can't you understand that? I love you."

"It's over. Don't you understand? Over. *Khalas*."

"But it can't be. I won't let it. Not yet."

"Over."

A dog howling, while the rain came bigger, faster.

"I love you. *Ahebaka*."

"Well, I don't love you. Not anymore."

A dizziness began to circle, and he clung to a muddy root.

"You don't?"

"No. It's over, I tell you. Over."

"Then I'll kill myself. I swear it. Kill myself."

"You're crazy."

"I'll kill myself. You'll see. You'll be sorry. You'll see."

"You're crazy. *Inte maynouna.*"

The dizziness stopped circling, landed, and he pitched forward, the vomit gushing. The voices stopped. With vomit steaming around his knees, Peter Spears jumped up and started to run. The rain whipped at his face, the vomit warm on his legs. But running, and now he could see the lights of his house—right over there. His legs tried to hurry, but off to his left—he could no longer ignore it—a new light loomed out of the darkness. Its long yellow beam moved quickly, animal-like, silently across one of the side-streets. The football wound begged him to stop but his legs no longer cared. He could see her curtains, the warm glow of lamp.

Peter Spears stopped. Something like a dark army ambulance had arrived, its exhaust white, boiling into the night, the rain swarming in and out of headlights. His hair a pasty-wet across his head, his chest forever heaving. He stood caught in its headlights, its wipers pulsating back and forth, back and forth. . . . There was a small wait, and then the window slowly rolled down and a hand motioned for him to come closer.

Pay Day

Every day except Friday the bus that is not really a bus but a big van drops Siera and the others off at six o'clock and drives away only to return fifteen hours later to pick them up. Once off the bus that is not really a bus, they file past the guards who, like always, are busy smoking and sipping tea and neverminding them. As Siera walks by the newest, biggest building, a woman opens a window, sticks her head out and yells something down at him. He squints up. She motions for him to come up. He counts the windows, the third floor. He looks around to see if there is some mistake. The others never stop to look or listen, walking faster, heads down as if fighting some sort of gale. She motions again, harder. When he goes up, taking the stairs because although it is a new building the elevators aren't working, not yet but soon, she is in the hallway waiting for him.

"Yes, Madam."

"Coffee. I need some coffee."

She is a pretty woman but something is wrong with her lips; her lipstick is the color of grape juice. That, and she has done something to her eyes; they look bruised and tired. Getting coffee is not his job, never has been. But he says, "Yes, Madam." He first goes down one hallway, then another, until he finds what is part coffee room and part storage boxes and brings her a cup, but when she sees it she insists on "More," and he goes back to the coffee room that is part storage boxes and pours her more and brings it back and this time she needs "Milk." He takes a deep breath, as if he needs new, bigger air, and this time leaves the coffee cup on her desk and goes back to get the milk and brings it to her but by now she is on the telephone, laughing big and purple, motioning for him to go away.

Before it is too hot, before the sea breeze grows milky and thick, Siera and two of the others will walk to the parking lot and begin picking up Coca Cola cans, plastic water bottles, ant-filled McDonalds papers, and stuff everything into large black garbage bags; after that, they will sweep the asphalt, pushing all the sand and dirt and gravel to the side, under the bushes and sometimes trees. This, according to the schedule, should be done by 8 a.m., 8:30 at the latest. By 8:30 it is too hot to be on the asphalt.

At 8:30 the schedule reads "water greenery" and they do. Starting with the small yellow plants that have always looked exhausted, near death, refusing to bloom even once no matter how much water they dump on them. After the tired plants, they snake the hoses over to the bigger, greener bushes, palms, and the neat row of flowers along the fence. By 9:00, all the watering done, Siera takes a special cloth and walks the stairs to the second floor and spends the next hour polishing, rubbing the special cloth over the rollercoaster of silver railing and banisters. As he rubs, he looks for spots, spots on the wall, on the floor, carpet. Any spots will do. After three years, two months, he has learned the importance of looking busy, staying in motion. He will rub and re-rub silver railing until it takes on a sheen that has almost nothing to do with silver, and all the while he will be thinking of how much money he must send home this month, the next three months.

His daughter needs new shoes, a dress, something for her birthday, school supplies, and how about his mother who isn't feeling well and needs a doctor, and, in the end, probably medicine. Rubbing that same section of silver railing.

Ten to 10:15 is break time, when Siera and the others go to the shed that is up against the back fence, near the garbage containers, where more hoses are coiled, where the leftover bricks and lumber and broken masonry is stacked. They slip off their sandals, lie flat on the cool cement and smoke and talk about last night or the night before. Their boss, a man just like them only older, taller, his pockets bulging with cigarettes, cellphone, papers, a row of different colored pens, sticks his head into the room to see what is what. He looks at his watch, grunts, and is gone. This, they have learned, is a good sign.

It is now time to go room to room, emptying small garbage bags into big ones. Some of the rooms are locked, the garbage impossible to gather. The boss does not like this. The garbage must be collected at 11:00, the schedule says so, and locked doors should be opened—by someone. The boss is very clear on this point, and blows cigarette smoke out of his nostrils to prove it.

From 11:30 to 12:00 there are carpets to clean, ashtrays to wipe ashless, more railing to rub bright. Then there is lunch. And for the second time they walk to that same shed to get out of the sun and heat and sit on the floor, sometimes on the bricks, sharing chapattis, rice, chicken, and tea. Some last minute smoking before 12:30, and the schedule says the grass needs cutting, and after that . . .

Today is pay day, and in the end, at nine o'clock, their boss will stop them at the accordion-like door of the bus that isn't really a bus and check off their name and number and then, once all is right, hand them their 50 dinars for the month. “Next.” Once Siera and the others are back home, back in their rooms, he will take off his uniform that is a dark blue, like the deepest, darkest part of the ocean, and talk to the others about anything but work.

The Reluctant Terrorist

Mind your own business.

He taps his pencil on the table once, twice, and then says, "But there is one problem."

"And what's that?"

"One big problem."

Although he is not the biggest, strongest, or even smartest of the four, it is his apartment, his food, and most of all, his plan. He is wearing a t-shirt that has the letters NYC across the back. He hunches over the table like he is hungry, like he is waiting for food, and says, "Yes, and what is that?"

"My sister."

Behind them and to the left is the TV showing some movie, a Western, and if they wanted to they could easily screech back their chairs, turn up the volume and listen to cowboys and Indians shoot at one another, one with guns, the other with bows and arrows; the cowboys yelling in English, the Indians screaming something in Apache, maybe Cherokee. If they wanted to.

You're not my boss. Never have been, never will be.

"My sister," he says again.

"And?" NYC asks for a third time.

"And she goes to that school, and on this day, this Tuesday, she will be there."

The four of them are hunched over the table, looking down at a paper that covers the tabletop; it is the plan they have worked and reworked for months now, and it goes something like this: the Mercedes will stop here, next to the weakest part of the wall, where there is more dirt than sidewalk, more weeds and trees than the stuff of wall, and then Ahmed, who is eighteen but looks older, will slowly get out of the car and lift the hood to see what is what. Of course engine trouble is everywhere these days, even with Mercedes: water hoses bursting, carburetors coming undone, something is always giving up with cars and engines. On this next part NYC has coached Ahmed; he must lean in and poke at the engine, turn his head first one way then the other, but the poking part is important. Finally, giving up, he will leave the hood gaping mouthlike and walk to the other side of the street; as he walks he will take out his cellphone and talk to nobody. All of this for the security cameras. Still talking to no one, he will continue on until he comes to the park and there he will sit on the stone bench that will allow him to watch all. Then, just as the students are filing in, the buses lining up at the gate and the two policemen, who really aren't policemen but wear uniforms and carry radios and holster revolvers that may or may not be loaded, slowly begin to make their way towards the Mercedes, when everything is just right, Ahmed will stop talking to nobody and push the button that they mean business, have always meant business, and that no one is innocent these days, and that America and all its soldiers and weapons and arrogant politicians will know that no one is safe. It will be a terrible but wonderful blow.

I'll see who I want to see, talk and walk with anyone I choose.

There is a long silence, and two of them unhunch to get a better look at him.

"Tell her to stay home. You're the older brother. Tell her she must do as you say. Stay home," announces NYC.

He taps his pencil to this. He knows Fatima will not listen to him. These days his no's become her yes's. She will argue with him, demanding why's. She believes arguing is all part of being Western, American. Although his groan is long and silent, he can't help but glance to see if they have heard. NYC runs his fingers through his hair and thinks the problem is solved, is easy, and he is not much of a man, let alone a brother, if he cannot control a younger sister.

"It is more complicated than that."

NYC laughs. "Tell her to stay away on Tuesday. It is easy. Tell her it is for her own good."

The other two decide to laugh at this too.

This hijab is choking me, killing me; I can't breathe, I tell you. Can't breathe.

Now that things are settled, they slip back into quiet, with plan and cowboys and Indians and small wooden table. The explosives are guaranteed to rip through the school wall, shattering the trees and assorted shrubbery. Nails, rocks, gasoline and parts of Mercedes will obliterate all within fifty meters.

In the beginning it had been all cards and *shisha* and coffee, and then, sometime in October, a friend of a friend introduced him to NYC who played *kout* better than any of them, who had more good ideas than bad. In October he never meant to plant a car bomb next to a school but NYC seemed so right and sincere that by February, when the meetings had grown to twice a week and some of the others had disappeared, leaving only the four of them, he knew it was too late. Meanwhile, Fatima had grown bolder, angrier, staying out late, reading English magazines, thinking MTV was freedom. She had become part of NYC's good ideas. Sitting at the table, he could see that now. He had waited for this night to tell them about Fatima, thinking, maybe, things would change, but nothing has changed. NYC has guns and explosives and friends with money, and Fatima. . . . Nothing has changed.

By now the Western is almost done, the cowboys done shooting, the Indians done dying. If the four of them were to stop, turn around and look, they would see the cowboys, their work complete, riding off into something like an orange sunset. But of course they don't turn, don't look. As he returns to the plan, he thinks of Fatima and his mother. Fatima because so much of this is her fault, and his mother because if she ever finds out, discovers the truth, she will kill him. Maybe she will borrow the *bakala* man's secret pistol, or late one night use one of her many kitchen knives. But if she ever finds out she will kill him—of that he is quite certain.

The Recruit

There is talk of instituting a mandatory two-year military service for all 19-year-old boys. This, the government says, would demonstrate the patriotic will of the young.

"They say at least ten. They say Suliman's brother got out with ten—five from each side."

General nodding all around.

But then he leans forward, elbows on knees, and in something just a little more serious than a whisper, says, "But to be safe better make it fourteen, fifteen even better. And make sure they're some of the big, important ones up front," grinning to show him what the big important ones up front look like.

At first he thinks it is a joke. Ever since they were kids, heroes together, Mohamed had always been that way. "Don't walk so straight. Don't you know anything about *jinns?* Like this, walk like this." Stumbling through the dusty street like somebody's drunken grandfather. "Like that. See?" Or, how about the time he insisted they hold their breath every time they drove through a tunnel "so the bad fumes can't get you," or that time last spring when he put the love note on his car, under the wiper, and signed it Your Mysterious Lover, a long line of hearts dripping down the page. So when he whispered, "Save yourself, get rid of the teeth," Abdallah watched for the slightest hint of joke, that tiny ripple of cheek flesh that almost always gave it away as a prank or trick. But when no dimple appeared, he says, “Say that again.” And Mohamed does, but this time leaving out the Suliman’s brother part, and still no hint of a joke.

In fact, Mohamed folds his arms across his chest and in a very un-Mohamed way, waits. This is different.

“Why at least 15 teeth? Isn’t two or three more than enough? Maybe two?”

“Regulations. Everybody knows that.” Letting his arm-folding come undone. “Has something to do with having enough teeth to aim a rifle, pressing your cheek hard against the metal, holding the rifle just right, arranging your head just so to get off the best shot. It’s been researched, you know. Studies. University studies. There is a relationship between teeth and aim. Everybody knows that.”

Nodding.

Samih, another friend but nothing like Mohamed, stops nodding long enough to run his fingers along his jawline, poking here and there.

“When do you report?”

“Soon.”

“When?”

“Two days.”

“Two days to save your life. Two days to take your teeth and save your life. This is a good trade off, *Sah?* A very good trade.”

Running his tongue over his teeth, secretly counting.

“Two days. There is time.”

The barber has a friend who knows a trick about taking out teeth, a trick that is cheap, painless, and fast. So by nightfall there is general agreement, and telephone calls are made and they go to the barber’s friend’s house that is a short taxi ride, just this side of the National Mosque.

"But I don't know if I'm ready. I mean, really ready."

That's when Mohamed holds up a hand, as if there's traffic to tame and he's there to do it. "Ready? What's to be ready about?" His hand holding back the traffic. "Ready? We're talking about your life. Abdallah, your life. What are teeth to life and death?" Now slowly lowering his hand, so the traffic can start up again. "Get in."

When they arrive it is too early and the barber's friend isn't there. His wife comes out and says he has gone to the airport and will be right back. "Back immediately." The three sit in the courtyard to wait; meanwhile, she brings them tea and dates and reminds them that he will be back soon, using both arms in wide sweeps to show them soon, and then goes back inside, locking the door behind her. They sip and look at one another and hang their heads as if they have been running a long race and now, with the finish line in sight, they are tired. They are almost waited out when Mohamed tells them a joke about camels and chickens that could have been funny at another time if there hadn't been so much waiting involved. Samih busily flips and reflips a leaf with the toe of his shoe. Finally, in a flurry, the barber's friend enters through the gate, says hello, and continues into his house only to return immediately with a paper sack. Everybody shakes hands, *As-salaam alaykuming, Wa alaykum as-salaaming.* Once he is ready and has lifted something out of the sack, unwrapped that same something from a brown cloth, he says, "Who is the patient?" Mohamed and Samih together, as if rehearsed, motion towards Abdallah, and the barber's friend nods as if this is a good choice, and asks Abdallah to "Please take this chair." And he does, all the while Mohamed is smiling and even gives him a fighter pilot's thumbs up.

The barber's friend has the hands of a laborer, gnarled and walnut-like, and he asks Abdallah if he is ready, and he says he is, and oh by the way, "You want ten teeth extracted, is this right, ten? *Sah?*"

"Fifteen," says Mohamed. "Especially some of the big important ones up front. But fifteen. Fifteen is best."

There is some more general tinkering of metal from the paper sack and when all is ready, he says, "Open. Wider, wider." He does.

"Take this."

"What is it?"

"Medicine. Don't drink it, just hold it in your mouth and swish it around."

Abdallah sips and swishes. It burns.

"More."

Sipping, swishing and burning.

"More." His mouth can hold no more.

"Hold it."

And he does until the burning goes away, leaving behind a big watery feeling.

Finally, "OK spit. Over there. In the flowers. Spit."

Mohamed and Samih looking hard at the spitting place.

"Fine. Now open. Fine. Wider."

What happens next is swift, and not at all the pain he had braced for. There is a line of small cracking sounds, the sort of cracks you hear when you bend the ice tray to get the ice cubes out, just like that only louder, faster, one right after another.

Once the barber's friend is done, wiping his hands on his pants and paid—Mohamed giving him something extra for fifteen teeth—it is still too early for the pain and Abdallah jokes and laughs with the others. Before they leave he asks Abdallah if he wants his teeth, jiggling them in his two hands like they are coins. Samih says, "Yes, of course." The barber's friend pulls a leather pouch from his jacket and drops the teeth in. As they walk back to the main street, his arm now around Mohamed, Abdallah thanks him. "It was a wonderful idea. How can I ever thank you? You saved my life."

"Nothing. It's nothing. You would have done the same for me. The very same." Smiling.

His face is still swollen and sore when he goes to report to the ministry two days later. Mohamed and Samih would go with him, if they could, but there are cousins to visit, carburetors to adjust, mothers and sisters to take shopping. Abdallah gets off the bus, walks to the biggest, brownest building, and after asking twice for the right room, finally finds it. There is a line of young men just like him, only bigger, thinner, shorter, fatter. There is a soldier with rifle in the room and Abdallah holds out the sheet of paper for him to see, to take, to examine. But the soldier does nothing like that. Instead, he tells him to go over there and take off his clothes and get in line. "Over there," motioning with his helmeted head. When his turn comes, he shows them his papers and without looking up they tell him to get in line again but then looking up for the first time, one of them in an especially white lab coat says, "Wait, what's wrong with you? You don't look so well. No. Stand up straight, that's right. What's wrong with your face?" The boy behind Abdallah—all sideburns and yellowing underwear—leans in to get a closer look.

"I lost some teeth."

"Let's see."

Abdallah holds his swollen face closer.

"I mean open your mouth." Meanwhile, all sideburns and jaundiced underwear has not stopped peeking over Abdallah's shoulder. "Wider, wider." The man with white lab coat squints into Abdallah's mouth. "What happened?"

"An accident. Bad accident," and he tries smiling through the swelling.

"Yes," and he writes something on a yellow form and gives it to Abdallah, saying, "Get back in line."

Once back in line everything goes surprisingly fast: pulse, blood pressure, "Cough. Again," an eye chart with no E's or B's, and then, at the end, another blood pressure, just to be sure. Someone like a sergeant, maybe a colonel, but anyway with three medals on his uniform, one gold, two silver, waits at the final table and when enough young men in underwear have gathered, he ushers them into a carpeted room where they raise their right hand and face the flag and promise to protect their country. The sergeant-colonel congratulates them on a job well done, and then points, "That's the way to your clothes."

On his way out, heading in the direction that the sergeant-colonel had pointed but getting lost and taking a wrong turn because he followed the rest of them, and with the yellow form still in his hand, Abdallah finds the first white-coated man and says, "Excuse me, but what about this?" waving the yellow sheet, "and this?" Opening his swollen mouth to reshow him where his once-teeth had been.

Taking the yellow sheet as if he has never seen it before, turning it over to see nothing on the back, "Yes, this is the yellow form for people like you. You know, the toothless, missing fingers and toes, harelips, cross-eyed. People like you. Congratulations."

"But what does it mean, this yellow sheet?" Now waving it like a small banner.

He re-takes the paper from Abdallah as if come to think of it this isn't yellow paper after all, not really, let me take a second look, but he just says, "Yes."

"There must be some mistake." Opening his mouth again. "Look at this? How can I shoot a gun? How can I aim a rifle? How? Impossible, don't you think? Impossible?"

"No mistake. The yellow sheet means no mistake. It means that once there might have been a mistake but not now; the yellow sheet means there's really no mistake at all. It's really very simple. Next?"

The Night Watchmen

According to local superstition a woman is guaranteed pregnancy if she can jump over the keel of a newly-built boat. On the other hand, it is said that if a woman were to do such a thing, that vessel would be doomed to bad luck. So, while the boat is being built, it is guarded day and night.

We're almost there. Around the corner.

Yes I know.

Quiet. You must be quiet.

I know.

Nothing, No sneezing, no giggling. Nothing.

I know.

"That's two."

"Two. Two what?"

Pointing almost straight up, "Shooting stars. That's two."

"Where?"

"There."

He bends to look and relook, then, "I don't see a thing."

Fishing for a cigarette, sighing, "Of course not, they're shooting stars. Gone." Showing him with his fingers how—poof—shooting stars suddenly disappear.

As the fire burns slowly, flickering, Hamad gently slips another piece of driftwood onto the fire, and sparks stitch into the night.

There it is. See it?

Of course.

If we have to we'll run and jump like we practiced.

Alright.

A little closer, and nothing, no giggling. Nothing.

Noura.

Alright, alright.

"How many nights is this now, six, seven?"

Ramy answers, "Five."

"Five nights, and how much longer?"

"Another week, they say. It's a small boat. Besides, what do you care, my uncle is paying us."

As the fire crackles, behind them and to the left looms the long, slender turtle-shell of the boat. It's nothing like a *dhow,* but bigger and better than a *warjiya.*

It is only after the tea is ready and poured that, "Hear that?" Both of them stop in mid-sip to listen. There is the breathing of the sea and beyond that somebody's husband screaming at his wife to shut up, at his kids to show him more respect, at the maid to "Don't just stand there."

"That?"

Hamad holds up one hand policemanlike to let him know that it's something else. More waiting until Hamad rises, taking one step toward the shadows just beyond the boat's hull. Ramy waits, watches, and after a while of nothing, stretching his hands out to the fire even though it is not cold.

"Cats."

What was it?

Wood. Twigs. I can't see.

You must be careful.

I will.

Wait.

Hamad returns to the fire, and when he does, both boys reach into their pockets and pull out cigarettes. "You think it was cats? It could have been. Some cat looking for fish. Maybe even a dog. It could have been a dog or a cat."

When the uncle had first warned them about this problem of girls, they listened, nodded, and finally looked at each other and snickered, thinking it was some sort of joke, but it wasn't, and the uncle, hands on hips, waited for them to stop. "Think it's silly, some sort of hocus pocus, wild bedouin talk? I tell you it's true, it works both ways, for the woman and against the boat. I've seen it. Heard of it. All true, I tell you. All true."

No more snickering, instead shuffling their feet in the sand, looking at one another, then back down at their feet, and finally at one another again.

Smoking and sipping and every now and again looking up into the moonless night and out at the twinkle of bluegreen riding the waves. The first night they had laughed and joked until sunrise. It was great fun to sit and guard such a small, unimportant boat and get paid for it. Night two there was only talk but no jokes and the sunrise was very slow in coming. Nights three and four were all cigarettes, *misbahas* and tea.

This time they both hear it, a click, the way a tea cup sounds when placed too hard on a tabletop. That, and something else, something like a blur of talk and laughter—giggling. Hamad looks hard toward the sound, in the shadows beyond the boat.

This time Ramy is the first to get up. Hamad, running his fingers through his hair, whispers, “See that. See that. I told you.” Ramy holds his cellphone out in front of him like a pistol.

Sshhhhh. I told you no giggling. Nothing.

I'm sorry, Noura. It just happened, came. Sorry.

Don't move. They won't come into the shadows. They're boys; look at them, boys. How can you giggle at a time like this? How? Don't move.

Ramy holsters his cellphone and gently steps toward the shadows.

Hamad does not move, whispering, “Ramy, wait. Wait. What time is it?”

Ramy stops, and half-turning, says, “What?”

“The time. What time is it?”

“Hamad, what . . .”

Fumbling with his cellphone, Hamad brings it up to his face, announcing, “Three twenty. It's three twenty.”

There is only the sea and the dying fire as the two boys look at one another. Finally, “Hamad, this is not Muscat, or Salalah, or. . . . This is different, you understand. We are different. It means nothing. Nothing at all.”

Seven months later, in the broil of a July afternoon, Ramy's uncle's small boat sinks. Survivors say, “One minute we were talking, joking, cellphoning, and the next the ocean was at our ankles; it happened that fast.”

Inshallah

"*Inshallah.*"

"You see there it is, that's the problem."

"It is?"

"Right there, that's the problem."

He has the slightest flurry of a moustache and something like a dirty chin for a beard; he stirs, blinking, "But, Sir, how? What?"

"That?"

He stops to look over his shoulder, as if there might be something on the wall, perhaps around the doorframe. "Sir?"

"*Inshallah,* God willing."

Sitting straighter, taller, adjusting the hem of his *ghutra*, head scarf, just so, and as he arranges, looking into the window-mirror to get it right, he forgets all about me, flicking the wings of his *ghutra* this way and that, placing them first off, then on his shoulder.

"Ahmad, you need to come to class. You need to do the homework. You need to hand in your work on time. I can't help you, I can't do my job if you're not there."

He is back now, his arranging all done. "Sir, I understand, but sometimes it is difficult because as you know the traffic is so bad in the mornings, and everybody is in a hurry and there is only so much road and the traffic lights care nothing about my being late; or, at the last minute, just as I am at the door, my hand on the doorknob, . . ." reaching out to show me how his hand is about to take the doorknob, " . . . and, Sir, out of nowhere my mother is suddenly there, insisting that I do an errand, drive to my uncle's, go to the store, take my sister to school, something that can't wait, she says. Then there was that one morning last week, Wednesday I think, when it was so windy and I had a cold and a headache, and maybe the flu. My eyeballs hurt, and. . . ."

It's the most talking he has done all semester, and I let him go on because I want to hear his voice, not just the yes, no, but real sentences. I wait to see how far he will go and do nothing but nod along with an occasional "I see."

" . . . And besides, this is all new to me, this university life, so please give me time to adjust, to get it right. Just a little more time, Sir."

In the end, "Yes, I get the idea, but you have already missed too many classes, far too many. You need to come."

"Yes, *Inshallah*."

"There it is again, you see?"

"What, Sir?"

"What you said."

"What is that, Sir?"

"*Inshallah*."

"Yes, *Inshallah*."

He sighs and turns to take a good look at my bookcase. I follow his gaze, and it seems to be especially interested in the second shelf, the row of Ibsen, Miller, Pinter, Shakespeare, Sophocles. I give his gaze a chance to wander, but when it doesn't, "You enjoy drama, Ahmad?"

"In high school we read *As You Like It*. I will never forget it. Never. But you know, I've never seen a bookcase like this. Seven shelves, is it? Big, very big." He pets his chin, and his *ghutra* slowly unfolds from his shoulders.

There is a silence, followed by some distant popping, then laughter. Not too far away the secretary is on the telephone, and her door is wide open and I can see her talking, looking at her computer screen and talking.

I pick up a pencil and look hard at its pink eraser. "But Ahmad, you have to take responsibility, you and you alone. It is your responsibility to be on time, to do your work, not God's. It doesn't work that way. If we all thought that way, God's will, then we wouldn't have to take responsibility for anything. God decides this, God decides that. You're off the hook, you see? We all are. Nobody's to blame. *Inshallah.* You fail a test. *Inshallah.* You forget to study. *Inshallah.* You see? Take control, Ahmad. Don't be afraid to take control."

He looks back at the bookcase, then back at me, and finally a new place, to my right and up, out the window and into the morning. "But what can I do, Sir? If it is the will of God, what can I do? Please tell me, what's to be done?"

I turn to see what he sees, and together we watch the whitecaps with oil tanker in the Gulf. When we finish he works his mouth, readying his lips, as if the words are all lined up and ready to come out. But then, at the last minute, he seems to change his mind, saying, "Yes, well. Perhaps it's something you cannot understand."

I look hard at him to see if I should be angry. But his one is not like that. He can't make it to class on time or remember when assignments are due. He is all cellphone, cigarettes and sunglasses. But he is not the other.

Back to rubbing the dirty newness of his beard, and when he turns to look again at the bookcase, I help him by saying, "I guess we're done. I just wanted to let you know about the situation, that's all. The situation."

Very quickly, like a kind of secret release mechanism, he stands, thinks about shaking my hand and then finally does. I end with, "See you in class tomorrow."

It's hard to tell, but as he is walking away, past the secretary who is still on the telephone, staring into the computer screen, somebody, somewhere whispers, "*Inshallah.*"

The Bank Teller's Tale

He'd seen it before, sometimes in supermarkets and department stores, once in a restaurant, but almost always in banks: the way two grandmas will be standing in line, minding their own business, waiting their turn, and then slowly, magically, they'd spy one another and start talking, forgetting all about waiting in line until somebody finally has to remind them to move up, "You're next." When that happens, the two grandmas will look up, half-startled, maybe even a little confused to find themselves standing in line, in a bank. And so, when the two of them fold their arms and turn to talk, he knows it won't be long before someone will have to remind them about being in a line.

Because it's a warm Tuesday in April, and because he'd just finished reading a story about a woman who lost both legs in a fiery car crash, he's feeling especially healthy and lucky. Meanwhile, the two grandmas agree that they both like springtime, and don't mind the heat at all. "It's really not hot. Warm, yes, but never hot." The taller grandma, the one with the bluewhite hair, nods. "Certainly." He smiles and looks down at his legs, the dirtyblack of his shoes. It is then, as he thinks about grandmas and having two perfectly good legs, that his gaze wanders to the big stylized wall clock, to the Amir's portrait, to photographs of past bank presidents, and finally to the tellers. Teller number two.

She could be twenty-one, twenty-two, maybe older, it's hard to tell when they wear their *hijab* like that: oval tight, choking off any hint of hair. But there's more: he's never seen such a white face—the way it shines like somebody's good idea of a full moon. The man at her window—an untucked blue shirt, with hair the color of baked bread—is talking, motioning with his hairy hands. She listens, nodding when he stops talking. Her face shimmering silky, she works her machine and gently, one dinar at a time, lays out his money. With the two grandmas having already forgotten about being in line—talking about intelligent grandchildren and birthdays, the taller grandma flicking her fingers to help her talk—teller number two deals with her next two customers just like that: silently, sadly mechanical.

He turns to watch her closer, harder. What has to be a Filipina, older, with short professional hair, moves to the window; like the others, she too talks and gestures, shifting her weight first this way, then that. Teller number two is quiet, only nodding when the woman's hands are done. All the while he's trying to understand why on a Tuesday afternoon, with the weather almost hot, and not a one of them dead or crippled, she would want to be this way, this silent indifference that looks and feels like a kind of unhappiness. She works her machine and opens her drawer and pulls out more dinars. Not once has her face stopped shining cool and porcelain. Now that he's edged a little closer, he can easily see her face, the way her cheekbones pushpull at her face. Her thin fingers neatly folded, she waits for the next customer.

The grandmas are next. They haven't noticed that they're next, but they are, and the one with the bluewhite hair is telling the other about her neighbors: "Germans straight from Germany," and how their cat is as big as her handbag—bigger—and the same color, too. But it's their turn, and the other teller—a tall man with a goatee—is saying, "Ladies." But she isn't quite done with the Germans and their cat, and so he has to lean out of his window, saying louder, "Ladies." Together they hear him, and now see him, and there it is, that surprised look, that look that says "what's a bank doing here?" Her cat story still unfinished, the two of them step toward the goateed teller.

Teller number two is waiting for him. Her hands are folded on the marble counter and her eyes are closed. He steps to her window and she opens her eyes. He says, "Hello." She nods and waits for him to say more, to do more. He slides the deposit slip with check across the cool marble. He says he'd like to deposit this please. Unexpectedly, nothing happens; she does nothing. In a small panic, he rubs his chin and tries thinking about what he didn't say, what he should have said. The grandmas are at the next window, talking strawberries and peaches and. . . . Just as he readies himself to say it again, she takes his check with deposit slip and fits them into her machine. As she turns to push buttons, he can see her necklace—some kind of jade animal swinging back and forth. He secretly tries leaning without leaning to get a better look. But there's more, because now he can see how her fingertips are red, how her fingernails are square and mannish. She is wearing a silver ring on her tiny finger.

She pushes the buttons quickly, without really looking at the machine but just above it, along its steel rim. Her lips are thin and tight, and around the rim of her *hijab* peek wisps of black hair. When she hands him the slip of paper that says his deposit is complete, thank you very much and have a nice day, all he can do is take the paper and say, "Yes, thank you." But before he gives way to the next customer, before he walks out of the bank and into the good heat of a Tuesday afternoon, he hesitates. Holding the receipt like it's a ticket, as if he's just bought a ticket, he waits. It is then, for the first time, that she looks him straight in the face. Her eyes widen, asking, Is there something else? With eyes still watchful, she reaches up to pull her *hijab* tighter, safer, and now finding the peekaboo wisps of hair she gently tucks them back. With the springtime and the Tuesday and both his legs working fine, he says as quietly as he knows how, "You look beautiful today."

Her eyes grow bigger, harder, and now something like a quivering moves around her lips, across her nose, and again she feels for any stray hair, her fingers doing a quick search, and when she does he can clearly see her jade necklace and its carving—a horse.

At the door he has to step around the two grandmas who have decided to stop and finish their talk—about goldfish. His heart is pounding and he feels a schoolboy embarrassment. Once in his car, feeling the heat on his back and legs, things are better, and yes, it was a good idea. As he starts the car, gripping the steering wheel, there is a tapping at the window. It's not even a tapping really, more of a pecking. He jerks to see. It's her. His first thought is a question: How can she do that? How can she walk away from her bank window just like that? He hurriedly does two things: rolling down the window, saying, "Listen, I didn't. . . ." But she doesn't let him finish, and with her fingers resting on the glass and her jade horse swaying, she leans over and angrily, frowning, as if he's the one who started it, he's to blame, says, "When can I see you again? When? *Meta?*"

The Ballad of the Retired Hangman

It was just like in the movies: black-hooded, feet firmly planted on the scaffold, arms folded across the chest, biceps not really bulging but the arm-folding helped.

He had been the city hangman for some twenty-two years, his father twenty-seven, his father's father almost thirty-two. His grandfather had been especially notorious for his relentless smile and untimely jokes; back then he wore something like a Zorro mask. His father had the same smile but knew nothing of jokes. "By God this is serious business."

His home, his father's home, his grandfather's, had once been on the edge of the city—houses to the north, rolling sandy hills to the south—but over the years the city had stretched until now his home was surrounded with busy roads, flashing lights, a crisscrossing of telephone wires. Still, the city couldn't disguise the fact that he was the hangman and it was his house—the hangman's house. Mothers threatened to drag their children over to the hangman's house if they didn't mind, do their chores, finish their homework. In the summertime when the evenings were sticky-hot, boys would sometimes sneak up to his house, just the other side of the hedge, and throw stones, twigs at his front door to show their buddies what courage was all about, and then run off into the night, arms raised in victory.

In the end, he had learned about nooses, making sure the knot was good and tight and placed under the left ear because the snapping always works better there; and although he wore a hood and dull workmen clothes with black boots, he knew his stuff, everybody said so. That, and he had made it a point to save all the nooses. It was bad luck to use the same noose twice. Everybody also knew that a used hangman's noose was charmed, and if used properly, carefully, almost always brought good luck. They say it worked on the same principle as rubbing a hunchback's hump. He kept his nooses in a steamer trunk in the closet, behind her long, once-worn dresses. A stack of roiling twists and turns of brown and wheat-colored ropes.

The grocer, two streets over, two shops down from the cinema, was the first. For a grocer he was too young, his hands too small and womanly. As a rule, grocers had always been older, bearded, storytellers; grocers always laughed the longest and loudest. He had wanted an entire noose.

"That will be costly, my friend. An entire noose?"

"Well yes, how much is it?"

When he told him, the young grocer's hands twittered around his chin and lips until finally, "That much?"

"Yes."

"How about a noose for two or three days. Can I rent a noose?"

The hangman had never heard of such a thing and laughingly told him so. Being serious and young, the grocer didn't like being laughed at; and besides, he was tired, day after day of getting up at four o'clock to open the shop for workers going into the city. He had no idea buying a lucky noose would be so difficult. "How about a piece of noose. A small piece?"

"How long?"

After some moments of thinking, rethinking, he settled on something about the length of a shoe, holding up his hands, "This long."

"Yes, we could do that. Certainly," said the retired hangman.

"How much?"

And he told him.

"Fine, I'll take that much rope." For the first time the young grocer smiled.

The hangman told him to wait, that he'd be right back, and, "Oh by the way, do you have the money with you?"

"Yes," the young grocer holding his hand against his pocket to prove it.

"Fine," and he stepped into his house, into his room that was really more than just his room but everyone in the family called it his room, and took the key that was around his neck and unlocked the steamer trunk that sat like a sleeping animal in the closet. There, like a meeting of snakes, lay twenty-two years of nooses. He waited, looking down into the square of coiled ropes. Finally, on his knees now, and looking back once, twice, just to make sure the grocer hadn't decided to follow him, he reached down, feeling his way along the bottom until he found what he was looking for, pulling it out. He knew his nooses, his clients, and this, he had decided, would be the first to go. Holding it out at arm's length.

This one had been his first, a rapist from Goa. Maybe eighteen, no more than twenty. He had said it was love, she said it wasn't. For this first one, the hangman's father had watched patiently from the foot of the gallows, and even though he had nodded that everything looked good and go ahead, when the trapdoor flew open, the eighteen-year-old's head slithered through the noose, and he hit the ground with something like a crack, breaking both ankles. He had to be carried back up the stairs screaming in pain and renoosed, but this time the rope was too tight and he sputtered that he couldn't breathe. He hanged him a second time just like that, with broken ankles, the boy screaming that he couldn't breathe. So yes, this one must go first.

With the heat came another, a young woman who had heard from a friend whose uncle knew the young grocer, and so here she was, a baby on her hip, saying, "Can I see them?" The retired hangman had never thought of it as a kind of shopping, this looking for lucky nooses, but before he said no, he tapped the baby's nose, and said he'd be right back and disappeared into his house. He didn't know why he did any of that except that he did, and he did nothing special in the house except open the steamer trunk, look in, shut it again, take five giant steps that way, five giant steps this way, and go back outside to tell her, "No. That's impossible."

She nodded as if that was only right. She looked at the baby who looked back at her as if to say, What? Then she said, "Give me one."

When he told her the price, he readied himself for shock, outrage, but there was nothing like that, just, "Of course."

Hers was the gardener who sold opium and hashish when he wasn't busy gardening. What made it doubly bad was that he was arrested during Ramadan, and he confessed to being sorry and said so on television, in the newspapers, for he needed the money to feed his family, four boys and two girls. Looking straight into the camera, "Four boys and two girls. What's one to do? Tell me? What can I do?" But the court didn't care for things like that. They waited until after Ramadan to hang him. The retired hangman had done everything right on this one. The noose was good and tight, the knot to the left to get the snap just right, but when it came to hanging time the gardener wouldn't die. He twisted and turned like one of those rodeo horses, kicking for five, six minutes, and even then when he stopped, the doctor with stethoscope said no, his heart was still beating. They waited eleven minutes for him to die. Part of his job was to stand there and watch, wait. Although it was just one of those things that had nothing to do with nooses and hangmen, just muscular necks, he felt bad about it. He sold the eleven-minute noose to her.

Four, maybe five days later an entire family came to his door, husband, wife, boy and baby. But there they were, huddled around the front door, and, "Excuse me, sorry to bother you, but we have heard about your good luck charms, the nooses, the grocer told us, and we have come to buy one if that's OK. We need it quickly. Just one."

"Yes, I understand."

They waited, unsure of what the proper procedure was. She was veiled, the boy more interested in the retired hangman's cats that had risen from their places in the shade to see what was what, and when the boy squatted, holding out his hand, the cats hurried toward him. The mother said, "Stop." But of course it was too late, the cats sniffing, nibbling at his fingers.

Their noose was a woman's who had murdered her husband, her husband's lover, and two assorted bystanders. She had a pistol and shot extremely well, almost soldierly, except for the two bystanders. On the gallows she refused the hood. Didn't need it. Said she wanted to see everything. "Everything. Even you," looking hard into his hooded eyes. He said, "Sorry, but it's the rule." Only then did he see her laugh. He hanged her on a Sunday, in a dust storm, and even though you can't keep a killer like that around, he felt sorry for her anyway. The woman, mother of two, killer of four. He sold the family the noose at a discount, and told them so, and they thanked him until he was tired of hearing their thanks. Once they were gone the cats slowly went back to their shade.

That winter a pimply teenage boy showed up at his door. He said he was desperate for something like good luck, and he had heard about his nooses and he needed good luck "real bad" and he had some money but not much but was willing to do almost anything for some good luck, and so on. While he listened to the boy, the retired hangman thought he would have some fun with this one, and so he asked him why he needed good luck, a noose. Since the boy wasn't ready for such a question, he hadn't practiced an answer, and the best he could do was look down at his hands and then over at the cats who looked back at him like they too were interested in his answer and then finally at the hangman's newly-painted green door.

"Well?"

"I just do. I'll pay anything for good luck. Anything." And of course the hangman knew he didn't really mean that, not really.

Smirking at this, the hangman continued, "Are you in trouble?"

"Who me?"

The hangman gazing up into his lemon tree.

"Me?"

That's when the hangman looked harder, closer at him, at the pimples around his mouth, the patches of hair that were trying their best to become something like a beard. Suddenly, it was no longer funny, and just like that he sold the Canadian's noose to him at a special discount. When the boy held the noose and saw the old blood stain, he asked what it was, and the hangman said, "Paint."

The gray noose had been a Canadian's, a clean shaven blonde man who they said had done it all: murder, drugs, rape, preaching the Bible—everything. This one cried the longest and the loudest. Said he was sorry, "Really sorry." There was blood on his noose; he had squirmed so hard that the rope tore his throat open. They said he died a kind of double death.

He had heard rumors about his good luck nooses. How one of his buyers had won the lottery, another had been promoted to store manager, someone else was almost run over by a truck but at the last moment slipped and fell into the ditch, unhurt. Somebody's grandmother didn't die even though doctors said she would. And so on.

He didn't miss his job, how could he. Sipping coffee, smoking, and stretched out in his chair, in his room, reading the morning newspaper, and then later, visiting old friends, only to return home to eat lunch and reread the paper. He took naps. So no, he didn't miss his job, and yet now that retirement had arrived it wasn't all they said it would be. In fact, in between the smoking and sipping and talking and rereading and napping, he fumbled around in his steamer trunk as if he had mislaid something, anything, and it was in there somewhere, if only he could take a closer look.

Evenings were for TV and the radio, for asking his wife what was for dinner, for questioning his children: "What did you learn at school? When will you be home?" But most importantly the evenings were for his friends, fellow retirees, a handful of neighbors. Of course there was drinking, a kind of too-sweet plum wine with beer, nothing serious. Almost always it wouldn't be long before they were lifting their glasses to ministers, old, forgotten colonels, assorted kings. They sang folk songs. *Shisha* for everyone. By the end of his first year of retirement he was down to half a steamer trunk of nooses.

So it went until the second spring of his retirement, that week she went to Syria. She wanted to visit her sister in Damascus. She would be back soon, two weeks, probably sooner, but maybe two weeks, and he was to take care of himself and there was plenty of food and Fatima could do all the cooking, cleaning, and again take care of himself, and he could always call her, and . . . In the beginning, when she came to him with her plan, her way was something between an asking and a telling; in turn, his way was to wave her away, "Go, go, leave. Leave me in peace." This, of course, would send her into a rage, screaming that he didn't care whether she lived or died. How could he. "How could you after all these years." Sobbing. He would roll his eyes and say, "Don't be silly. Go." After a long brooding silence where she went outside and then came back inside and then went outside again, she happily said, "Alright." For fifteen years this had been their way. So one April morning, with the birds almost too loud in the lemon tree, she, with children, went away to visit her sister in Damascus. He went to the door and held up his hand as they drove away, which was his way of saying good-bye.

It happened three nights later. It was extra warm, even hot for April, and his friends had come to celebrate his loneliness. Like always there was drinking and remembering old bosses and older lovers, and then laughter, recalling the time . . . By now the retired hangman had put his feet up on the bench next to the lemon tree, and as he threw his head back to laugh long and hard at Ghazi's joke, he looked up into the tree's branches, and come to think of it, "You know, there was one customer, a raw sort of fellow from the hills, someone who knew nothing of law and order, just sheep and bad teeth, but still a customer, and it all started with a wedding that had gone all wrong; families were insulted, tribes disrespected and in the end two boys and an old man lay dead in the desert. It wouldn't have been so bad if it had been men, but two young boys and somebody's 87-year-old grandfather could not be tolerated. Of course he ran away before they could catch him, hunt him down, and probably kill him. But the soldiers heard about it and caught him and brought him back shackled. There had been a trial and families demanded satisfaction, even justice, no blood money would do."

When the retired hangman got to the hanging part, he showed them what a spooked, wide-eyed man from the hills looked like standing on the gallows. They slapped their knees and laughed, spilling plum wine everywhere. They wanted more. "Do it again. Show us again." The retired hangman saying, "I'll do it better. Wait. Just wait," and undoing his feet from the lemon tree bench, he hurried into the house, into the closet, opened the trunk and yanked out a long rope with noose, slipping it over his head. He reappeared, "Like this. See? See?" His eyes bulging funhouse. They roared with laughter. And so it went.

By now the moon was high in the lemon tree branches, and with the wine and beer all gone, they had had enough, and shaking hands all around they said good night as only late night drinkers can and disappeared into the darkness. Still noosed, the rope wagging behind him, the hangman went as far as the walkway, and with hand raised said good night. He grinned all the way back to his room, aaahing down into his chair, and fell asleep just like that, noosed, the rope winding between his legs.

He awoke with a start, in the dark, not remembering where he was. There was a noise. Someone at the gate? Frowning to listen harder, and yes, someone, something, at the gate, and now remembering, perhaps it was someone wanting to buy a good luck charm, a lucky noose. To say he ran wouldn't be right, because he hadn't run in years but he did jump up from his chair, and in something like a sudden shuffle, made for the door, the rope snaking across the floor behind him until it snagged on the heavy cabinet. Wide-eyed and thinking he had something to say, scream, he reached the open door just in time to feel the crush of rope around his throat, his head thrown one way, his legs the other.

When Fatima came the next morning to clean, make breakfast, she found him that way in the doorway; and because she was older, uneducated, and thought nothing of bigger things than cleaning and cooking and sending money home to her family, she never once thought of his terrible death as being the stuff of irony.

Rumors of Midgets

Legend has it that some sixty or seventy years ago the first one was spotted in the city, which back then wasn't really a city, more like a fat town that was just beginning to know what oil was all about, and even then it wasn't really in the city itself but one of those suburbs with one foot in the desert. But now there's rumor of another one, somewhere in Salmiya.

When this second one was born, his parents, one of the older families that knows all there is to know about pearls, knew nothing of his midgetry. In the beginning there was nothing to fret about, all babies are small. Yet as he grew he didn't; everybody waited for him to catch up with the others his age, but he didn't, couldn't. So one day, they say, in the early morning heat of a Sunday in June, the mother with maid decided to take him to the doctor for tests, and sure enough after two or three weeks the tests results said midget. In public the family said everything was all right, people are different, God's will, etc. But in private, behind closed *abwaab,* they worried.

His name was Nasser. But for the most part it was just the midget who lived two streets behind the mosque, in the greenandwhite corner house. As Nasser grew but didn't he had a hard time making friends. Of course children made fun of him while everybody else stealthily tried not to stare. It seemed nobody wanted to be seen with a midget, no matter how cute or toyish.

Nasser had two older brothers who were not midgets. In fact, they were everything that a midget wasn't: tall, manly, loud. They say the two brothers loved their midget brother sometimes, at home, alone, but would never take him with them to the chalet, to the coffee shop, to the mall.

The mother begged them to take him but they said no, they couldn't because they were meeting friends, staying out late, because. . . . They always had to wait for him, his short legs constantly working overtime to catch up, sweating, his tiny chest heaving. Besides, the cigarette smoke wasn't good for him.

It wasn't that Nasser was completely unloved. They say his parents loved him more than the other two sons put together, and to prove it they bought him whatever he needed, wanted, dreamed about: toys, pets, bicycles that twinkled in the dark. That, and he had two Filipino maids, just in case.

On his birthday, fourteen, maybe fifteen—who can say when you're always that small—but his birthday for sure, his two brothers took him out into the desert as a present, somewhere along the Saudi border. Once there, they set up camp and pointed this way and that into the big emptiness and then, finally, that evening, turned to him, saying, "We'll be right back," and sped off into the starry night, leaving him next to the fire with tent and his favorite *Saluki.* They say it took him two days to walk home, to find his way. The *Saluki* was never found. When Nasser walked in the front door, his mother red-eyed from weeping, his father having not stopped grilling the older sons for two days, he shook the dust and dirt from his *dishdasha* and hair, washed his face, and after taking a long drink of cold water, turned to the brothers, who hadn't stopped looking down at their hands, at the floor, asking, "I thought you said you'd be right back?" They murmured that it was supposed to be something like a joke, a birthday joke, talking down at their feet. The mother wailed and squatted to hug Nasser properly. The father, roaring like some zoo lion, grounded the two sons for life, or the equivalent.

When Nasser grew up in the sense that has nothing to do with bigness, everybody decided that he didn't have to work but could stay home, surrounded by Filipino maids and bigger and better toys, not to mention his second favorite *Saluki.* He was a good boy, was Nasser. Everybody said so.

About this same time, as his brothers left the house to marry, to go off to the UK, to work for an uncle, Nasser, all alone now, began to change, some would call it overnight. He had grown weary of staying home, his best friends being the driver and the two Filipino maids, who, by now, treated him something between a son and a brother, and so enough was enough. He grew a full, unmidgetlike goatee, and when he went out—one of the Filipino maids shadowing him just in case—he did all the right things: sunglasses, cellphone, clutching a pack of cigarettes. He did everything he was supposed to do, only in a smaller way.

In the end, when his favorite maids decided it was time to return to Cebu, and the driver was almost never on time anymore and *Salukis* weren't as fun as they used to be, Nasser went away, to Europe, some place like Prague where midgetry is not uncommon, even expected. To this day they say his mother misses him, and will sometimes fly to Prague to visit him, say hello, bringing him videos of his greenandwhite house, his brothers—one leaning up against his new Humvee, the other tourist-like, with Big Ben in the background—and the father standing in front of the Stock Exchange, waving, smiling.

Math 212

The Ministry of Education has proclaimed that in the university, in the classroom, men and women should be separated, divided. Not only that, but to insure division some sort of barrier or barricade is recommended. In the long run, this is the best policy, the safest way to deal with men and women who might confuse learning with something else. So says the Ministry.

The math professor, a tall American who spends too much time believing he is special, moves first to their side of the room, telling a joke or two before announcing the answers to the quiz.

"Noura, what did he say?"

"A joke. Something about bald-headed men, I think. I don't know. Maybe something about men without heads. Anyway, a joke."

"What else? Something else."

"Answers to the quiz."

I lift my eyes as far as they will go, craning over the partition that separates us from them. He is jabbing his finger to make the point stronger, more important. He answers questions this way: pointing hard at students, chairs, the wall, as if to help the answer along. Done explaining, he slowly, like some sort of heavy boat rounding the bend, steps to our side, the women's side.

The partitions are on wheels, panels of milky, shower-door glass that, when arranged end to end, in a straight line, cut the classroom in half—them and us. If we turn and look just right, we can see the tops of their heads, bobbing, and every now again a peak of eyebrow, their dark bodies moving underwaterlike through the murky glass.

As a rule, they have more fun than we do, laughing, giggling, slapping one another on the back, and sometimes when he is at the board scrawling one of his mathematical formulas that fills up the board like an octopus, its tentacles going every which way, a wad of paper will sail over the glass. As a second rule, there is nothing written on these wads, just a sheet of graph paper, sometimes two, and if time permits and he hasn't stopped scrawling, we resail the paper back over.

He drifts back to their side, to the very corner of the room, the partition slicing him off at the neck. We have talked to him about this after class, this staying on their side, in the corner. Five, six, even seven of us will go up to him, arranging ourselves in a neat half circle, and tell him we can't see, hear. "Why do you insist on them? The boys. How about us?" He will say, "Yes, I understand," and nod. But he is from Houston, Texas, and maybe in Houston, Texas, there is something about men sticking together, about holding their own, maybe it has something to do with cowboys, I can't be sure.

Anyway, this is week five and midterm exams are nearing and sometimes Fatima, who is all about straight A's, is constantly waving her arm like she is flagging down a taxi to get his attention, to get him out of the corner and back on our side, or at least in the middle.

Two hands rise from their side, and he jabs at one of them, "Yes?"

It is a question about answer four. "Sir, is that correct? X = 23 is right?"

I can tell he likes being called Sir. In the beginning, Fatima called him teacher, and when she did he stopped in mid-talk, saying, he had worked hard for his PhD, six years and many a sleepless night, and he isn't just a teacher but a professor, and by the way, it isn't Mr. but Dr., etc. He assures the handraiser that number four is correct.

The class is half over before he launches into Chapter Five, and this, he says, "Is my favorite of all the chapters." Noura nods as if it is her favorite too. He clasps his hands together just under his chin like a kind of prayer and turns to them saying something about, "Affection . . . promise. . . . We shall see, right?" This is funny and they laugh, their heads bobbing violently.

"What?"

Noura shrugs.

With time almost up, he tells us again that this is his favorite chapter, and turns to explain the differences among obtuse, acute, and reflex angles. He does this in a flurry, his magic marker working furiously, all the while talking straight into the white board. When he finishes, a voice from their side wants to know what a reflex angle is.

I look to Fatima for help. "Who can that be? Who's talking?"

"Hard to tell. Maybe Hamad, or Nabil, one of the two. It sounds like Nabil, talking through his nose, asking questions like that."

For some reason he decides to look at us, insisting that, "I just explained that." He pokes his magic marker at the board, creating a line of green dots that have nothing to do with angles. Sara, in a mild panic because he is now looking right at her, quickly probes the rim of her *hijab* for any loose hair that might have crawled out. I look down, smiling straight into the tabletop.

With time up, he drawls, "Do pages 166-168, all the odd numbered problems. Any questions?"

But when I raise my hand, it is useless because their side is already up and aiming for the door.

In the end, Mohammed, Fatima, Abdullah, Noura, and I will, like always, meet in the coffee shop downstairs and gather around the big table in the back, and with jazz oozing out of the walls, we will talk about what he said and didn't say in Math 212.

East of Jahra

He should have seen it coming. Should have paid more attention to the sky, to the horizon, to the north. Storms like this always come from the north. But he did none of these things. Besides, all that doesn't matter now. What does matter is that it was her birthday, and as a present he'd given her one of those four-wheel beach buggies that almost all her friends had and she needed one, too. So he had done the right thing and bought her the newest model, in green.

Of course she has heard, too, how could she not. That's when she pokes her head out of the tent, saying, "*Shisalfa?*" But seeing that he is too far away and that the rain is coming down harder, bigger, she says it again, louder, "*Shisalfa?*" After all, as mother she has every right to say *What* whenever she wants. By now not only is he too far away, but running as well. She can't remember the last time she'd seen him run for anything, anyone. She leaves the tent, and never mind the rain and wind, but out of the tent, and at times like this, when husbands are running and the sky is exploding, who cares about *hijabs* and *abayas;* besides, they are in the middle of the desert, east of Jahra, with only a group of tents thataway—somewhere through the rain—and over there two SUVs side-by-side along the pipeline. The wind angrily sweeping in, she can see it coming, rippling over the sands, dust and dirt jumping out of the way, mashing her gown hard against her body, yanking her hair, witchy.

It all started with blue sky and just a hint of clouds the color of weak tea on the horizon. There had been laughter and happy fourteenth birthday from everybody, and of course the younger brother couldn't stop being mad because he wanted a buggy too, only red, and faster, bigger, better.

At first the father told her to "Sit here," and he drove to show her how. "See, push this, and this is the pedal here. See? Brakes." And all the while she never stopped saying, "Yes, I know. I know." But he had heard that before, and went on. "To turn off the engine, here. See?"

"Yes, I know."

In the end, he let her drive and she did know, driving as if she had done it before, many times before, and when they got back to the tent, they said happy birthday again and she said thank you again, hugs and kisses all around, but even he could see she'd rather be driving than thank youing, kissing. He didn't look up, didn't scan the sky but he's almost certain it was still sunny and bright, and so yes, "Go over there," pointing in the direction of nothing but Iraq, "and be careful."

"Yes, I know."

From then until the blinding flash with crackle he sat with his son on the plastic chairs outside the tent, listening to him complain. "Can I drive when she gets back? Can I? When can I get mine? When?" And so on. It was only when there was a lull in his complaining, after he had smoked three, maybe four cigarettes—letting them die red-eyed in the sand—that a darkness suddenly moved over him, and when he looked up, expecting to hear his wife, "*What are you doing? Where'd she go? When will she be back?*" there were only black clouds. *Sarayat.*

Standing up now to get a good look at north, the plastic chair losing its balance, thudding into the sand, he could hear her before he saw her, the chatter of the buggy. Then there she was, charging down the wave of a sand dune, coming this way. As she disappeared into the trough of the next dune, it happened: a bright white flash followed by a crackling, as if something big and important had snapped.

A splintering of air. It throws him to his knees. Recovering quickly like only a father can, he jumps to his feet, sand flying, looking to see, to find the noise, forgetting all about the complaining son, maybe even pushing him away, forcing him to the ground. That's when two things happen almost as if practiced: white smoke curling up from over there, where she has disappeared, while the wind and rain and sand are suddenly upon him, at his mouth, eyes, and nose.

There's nothing left to do except run toward her, the mother behind, gaining. Fighting the wind and rain, he finally makes the rise, and looking, seeing his daughter, a new fourteen, a friendly white smoke rising impossibly straight from her head. And just like a kind of ballroom magic, the black clouds are done, gone, the thunder and lightning throwing fits somewhere over the Gulf. *Sarayat.* Shreds of *abaya* flutter like tiny flags, curlicues of smoke rising from her fingertips, a kneecap, her hair sprawled black across the sand. One sandal on, the other sticking toe first out of the sand, a leather strap flapping. The green buggy is on its side, broken down the middle, one of its wheels still spinning as if it hasn't been told its driving is finished. Only now does he remember to call out her name, "Safaa." Almost there, "Safaa, Safaa."

The mother behind him but catching up, and now like something out of a cartoon, passing him, screaming loudest, her hands outstretched as if in someway that will help. Even as he runs, he, shamefully, is thinking ahead, thinking to the days and nights ahead; although he knows nothing of death and dying except from the stuff of TV and movies and one long-ago cousin, seeing the white smoke rising from her once head and feet, he knows, and her death will be nothing compared to the days and nights to come. Now it is his turn, and with a sudden burst, he rushes to pass the mother because he wants to get there first, before her, so he can . . . can . . . ?

When he arrives he is afraid to touch her because most of her head and legs are a butcher shop red, everything else an oily black, and all he can do is turn and try to stop the mother, push her away. The thunder and lightning, an angry bruise over the Gulf, and as he fights with her to stop, to keep away, trying to grab her wrists, he feels ashamed, as if so much of this, of everything, is his fault. If only he had looked skyward sooner.

Ancient Civilizations 101

He has been waiting in the shifting shade of one of those old dusty palms for what seems like hours, maybe longer—ever since she went in. The longer he squats, waiting, one cigarette after the other, cellphone at the ready, the weaker the shade grows, until finally he must stand, take one step back and re-squat to stay out of the sun. Meanwhile somebody's calico cat has wandered over to visit him. He pets it—not even petting, just one stroke along its bony back—and the cat wants more, won't go away until he's stroked it two, three more times. In the end, the sun too much for it, it slips back into its deeper, darker shade.

He watches as two women come out of the building, one laughing, the other with plastic bag, doing all the talking. Right after that, the two of them turning the corner, the plastic bag between them, someone else comes out, an old man wearing a suit and tie that is all wrong for the heat of midday. From the shade of the palm, he watches him move into the sunlight, first looking left, then right, as if there's a choice to be made. He struggles with sunglasses that refuse to let go of his coat pocket. Once free, he slips them on but they aren't done with him yet because they are crooked and he stands there with one eye higher than the other. Ready now, he decides on left, following the two women. It isn't long before the calico is back, and this time he doesn't touch it, not even a glance, but the cat won't stop rubbing against his leg.

Finally, it grows tired of doing all the work, and stops and starts its way back to its place in the big shade of the building. All the while Sherif never stops watching the lobby with elevator where she will have to come out.

Sherif had never been a bad boy, not like some of the others, even his sometimes friends, who drank whiskey, who toyed with drugs, who every now and again hated Americans when it seemed like a good idea. He was nothing like some of those with guns and alcohol, those who are used to getting things their way, insisting until they are red in the face. But this was different. Mariam was different.

In the beginning it had been just another one of those university classes, with girls on one side of the room, guys on the other, the soft clicking of *misbahas*, cellphones on vibrate, while up front, a tall bearded professor from Florida, who amazingly almost never glanced at his notes, lectured, pacing tiger-like. And so it went, like clockwork, Sunday, Tuesday, Thursday, one ancient civilization after another. Sherif sometimes took notes, mostly not, other times drew what he could see of her face, the smooth scoops of her cheeks, her long brown hair, the way she frowned when she wrote in her notebook, her tongue hard against her lips. When she turned just right, he could see all this. That, and he liked to watch the professor prowl from side to side, letting his hands do the talking, pulling down maps, charts and diagrams like so many window shades, jabbing at the white board as if Tutankhamun's tomb was there, right there.

But then there was that Thursday in November when she came in late, mid-lecture, and for the first time Sherif could see her clearly, away from the flurry of *abayas*, sunglasses, and backpacks. The professor, of course, never stopped, the Aztec civilization cared nothing about tardy students. Sherif watched her softly click the door shut, and then wait for him to stalk to the other side before taking her seat next to some blue *hijab*, pulling out her notebook and pen. But there is more, because later, the class almost done and Cortez having done his terrible duty, she raised her hand to ask a question. He remembers the asking but not the question because she just raised her hand and asked. None of this waiting to be recognized, given permission to speak. Aside from a once-in-awhile unimportant "Yes," "No," it was the first time he had heard her voice; and that night, watching the ceiling from his bed, he would think how it sounded exactly the way he imagined it would: direct, confident, unafraid. They all watched, waited, the professor holding out both hands, as if her question was right there and all he had to do was pull it in. He started to answer but then, after a "Yes, but . . . ," his hands, palms up, slowly seemed to change their mind, and after a short silence, followed by much beard scratching, he said, "I don't know. I can't answer that question." Even Sherif knew that professors didn't like saying things like "I don't know," "Not sure." How it was always better to make up an answer. Students demanded answers. Almost anything was better than "I don't know." Besides, how could a professor who almost never referred to his notes not know the answer? "Don't know." But she only smiled, closed her notebook, and nodded as if that was good enough. That was the beginning, seven months, three weeks ago.

This was the third time she had come to this apartment complex, the fourth if you count the time she almost went in but then, at the last moment, at the elevator, talking on her cellphone, didn't. And of course by now he is certain there is someone else. Someone with more money, a bigger car. Someone who no longer has to sit in a classroom and be reminded of the fall of the Roman

Empire. He had talked it over with his friends, Nawaf and Wahab, and they both agreed that it was bigger than the stuff of just boyfriend girlfriend; it had to do with respect and honesty, and so yes, "Something will have to be done," Nawaf had said, rapping his knuckles on the tabletop. There was a lesson to be taught, and as her boyfriend of seven months, three weeks, he was the one to administer it. This, they agreed, was only right.

Sitting there in the dying palm shade, the calico watching him from its shade, he thinks back to that night the three of them sat among coffee cups and *shisha,* and feels better, and to prove it he pulls out another cigarette, lights it and runs his fingers over his back pocket to make sure it is still there.

Finally, just as he is beginning to think the waiting has become too much, too long, the shade too weak, and that he will have to wait until next time to teach her a lesson, she comes.

Unsquatting, a faint popping somewhere in his knees but never mind because there she goes toward her car, walking too fast, which is a sure sign. She looks different, bigger, brighter, like that day she walked in late, asking an unanswerable question, nodding, smiling. This only makes it worse. He walks faster than he wants to catch up with her. At the car, her key aimed and ready to unlock, he grabs her by the shoulder, spinning her around—car keys flying—demanding, "Who is it?"

What comes out of her is more squeak than scream, which almost changes his mind, but then she says, "You."

"Who? Who is it? *Menow?* Giving her shoulder a shake, her sunglasses somersaulting thataway.

"What is wrong with you? Who? Who?"

"You think this is funny, a joke?"

This is the part that Nawaf and Wahab had warned him about. *No jokes. Don't let her off the hook. No smiling, no jokes. This is serious business, you understand? Serious business.* Wahab taking his turn to thump the tabletop with his fist.

Searching her face for signs of betrayal, something like a smudge, a fresh redness, disheveled hair, anything will do.

Looking for her keys, she sees them over there, leaning magically against the wheel, twinkling silver; she tries to pull free but his hand never leaves her shoulder, and with the other he reaches into his back pocket pulling out the scissors. "Who is it?"

"What's wrong with you?"

"Who are you seeing? *Menow?*"

Her almost perfect voice now recovered, daring him, just like they said she would: *Be stern. No matter what, stern is important.*

"None of your business."

"But it is my business. It is."

Trying to shrug off his hand and step toward her keys at the same time, and again he says, "You think this is funny?" With the same shoulder hand he pushes her head down.

"Stop. What's wrong with you?"

But enough is enough, and as she struggles he cuts, snipping, jabbing, bits and pieces of brown jumping into the air. He does it again and again, and as he does he can see her raising her hand strong and straight, asking her question, the other boys leaning forward to get a better looksee, followed by the professor's puzzled look, Ancient Civilizations 101. But snipping away, just like they planned: *A lesson she will never forget.* Globs of long brown hair jumping into the air. The snipping and gouging make her wild, and with a strength seen only in movies, her shove sends him sprawling. Half in blue flowers, half in dust, he can't believe she would do that to him, her boyfriend. Meanwhile, panting, staring down at the hair around her feet, all she can say is, "What? Why?" Tears and anger now, but he cares nothing for things like that and he is on his feet, his scissors snapping like some small creature that has nothing to do with him.

"Who is it, Mariam?" he demands. "Who lives here? Why are you so disrespectful? Everybody says so. Disrespectful. How could you?"

Staring at him, her fingers feeling her scissored hair, long brown strands coming away in her fingers, and for the first time he sees a face that is not hers, has nothing to do with her, but there it is. And she says, "My aunt. My aunt lives here."

Holding the scissors next to his chest, and of course he says, "No. You're lying." But seven months, three weeks is long enough to know she isn't; still, it is his job to say it again, "Lying."

Demand the truth. It's your right. The truth.

She looks up into his face, almost whispering now, "My auntie. Auntie. Who else could it be? Who?"

They had not talked about this; Nawaf and Wahab had not considered this, and as he lowers the scissors—the sun suddenly a white heat across his forehead—all that is left is remembering the bearded professor who had no answer to her question.

After the Music Lesson—Times Three

The Father

It starts with sobbing—nothing bigger; in fact, if I hadn't been there from the very beginning I might have thought it had nothing to do with tears but more of a muffled giggling—the way she jiggles and wiggles her shoulders. You know how little girls can be. But I had been there from the start; and peeking over my newspaper I saw the way she came in from the garage, flopping on the sofa, clicking on the TV, throwing something like a "*Marhaba*" in my direction. Meanwhile, her mother, hearing all, sticks her head out of the kitchen because it's Friday and Jenny has the day off. It was then, even before she could click to her favorite program, that the mother asks extra-loud, "Where's your clarinet?"

That was the beginning, and from then on it was a mix of tossing the remote on the coffee table, walking back to the garage, looking and relooking in the back seat, front seat, and even opening the trunk that hadn't been opened since *Eid*, screaming for Siera to come and make things right, and still no clarinet. This brings us to now and how the TV has been rudely turned off and how she is slowly pulling her wet face away from her wetter hands, and when she does she immediately decides to stare at the ceiling. She goes for the longest time without blinking. Her tears all finished for the time being, she finally gives up on the ceiling and looks down at her hands, turning them this way and that, like she's never seen them before.

"Where is it?"

Meanwhile, from the kitchen, the mother has not once stopped reminding her just how much a clarinet costs. The clanging of pots and pans, the way she rips off the top of the macaroni and cheese box, as she loudly, angrily prepares dinner, and now breaking one of her favorite glasses but not seeming to care because, after all, this daughter of hers has lost a clarinet, not just any clarinet, mind you, but Uncle Amer's favorite clarinet and Auntie Amal's before that, and . . .

It is all the daughter can do to stay on her feet. As a matter of fact, just when I decide I have had enough and start for the bedroom to find something else to do, anything else, I hear a thump, followed by what can only be described as a kind of swimming on the carpet. I don't have to look to know she has pitched herself onto the floor and is now thrashing about on the beige carpet like some American Southern Baptist.

"Your Uncle Amer's favorite clarinet, and guess what, he loaned it to you—to you, of all people. And what have you done?" Out of nowhere, a radish flies across the room, thudding red against the wall, rolling behind the TV. "What have you done? Lost it. Who knows what it's worth. Who knows."

That's when I change direction and head toward the back door and the garage and the car. I grab the flashlight that is supposed to never leave its hook by the door but of course is almost never there because somebody always forgets to put it back, or has left it under their bed, or put it somewhere else so they won't forget it. But this time there it is, dangling from its golden hook; and so thinking quiet is a good idea, I softly open the door and slip into the garage and open the car door that should be locked but isn't. I really don't need the flashlight because a starry twilight has found its way through the one tiny window, but I click it on anyway as I bend to take one last look under the seats. I hear Siera outside, along the street, talking, laughing, with the other drivers in the neighborhood. And naturally there it is, naked and out of its case, but right there like a kind of black femur, jammed awkwardly, almost impossibly up into the springs of the seat. Now using the flashlight in earnest, I carefully unwedge it, scraping it around the mouthpiece and just a little along its dark underbelly, but nobody will care about that—not now. Groaning up off the car floor that smells of popcorn and *shisha*. I lock the car and then rehook the flashlight because, after all, we don't want to lose it.

While I was away, she stopped thrashing long enough to vomit a long yellow line across the carpet—speckles on the coffee table and across magazines. Accordingly, the mother has come out from behind the macaroni and cheese to get mad at her a second time for vomiting on a beige that, as everyone knows, is almost impossible to keep clean. But even I can see she is looking deadly pale, and with the found clarinet still in hand, I help her back onto the sofa. Now remembering, I say, "Excuse me, but look what I found." Neither one of them looks right away, neither one believing I can possess anything of importance at a time like this. I know my family. Finally, grudgingly, they turn ever so slowly, and like a kind of magic, everyone is well and happy. She finds the strength to whisper, "Where did you find it?"

"Under the seat."

"But I looked there, once, twice. I looked there."

I nod.

The daughter is unsteady and still white across the forehead, along her neck, but sitting up now, feeling better, saying, "See, I told you I didn't lose it. I told you."

The mother, feeling better too, after all, a brand new clarinet can cost hundreds of dinar, answers, "Yes, well, good for you," before stepping back into the kitchen to click her tongue at the broken glass.

The young daughter takes the clarinet from my hand and feeling so much better now, with a new lively color beginning to seep back into her face, looks the instrument up and down just to make sure, and that's when she stops, leans closer, and then, showing me the kind of anger she's been taught, growls, "You scratched it."

The Mother

Macaroni and cheese. I'm in no mood for steak, and certainly not spaghetti, her favorite—not now. "Nur, think! Where could you have left it? Where? At school? How about on stage, behind the piano? Did you look there? Did you? Did Siera bring it in? Maybe Dalal took it by accident. Did you call Dalal?" *Why does Jenny stack the pans like this?*

"Yes, I looked everywhere. Everywhere."

There goes a glass. Our anniversary two, no three years ago. Snapped off at the stem. "Nur, think!"

Stepping to the refrigerator she spies a bowl of last night's radishes; she grabs the biggest, reddest of the bunch and . . . *There, that's better.*

She stops to look at her thumb: a perfectly straight red line. *Glass. Not even worth a band aid.* She wipes her thumb along her waist, thinking since she's in the kitchen that she must be wearing an apron, but she isn't. *And now there she goes: throwing her fit. Making a proper fool of herself. Well let her, serves her right. Now where's he going? Just like him not to say a word, nothing like a reprimand, always sneaking out the back door. Macaroni and cheese, nothing more. Serves both of them right. Once Amer finds out I'll never hear the end of it. "You know how much one of those old ones costs? Any idea? I didn't think you'd lose it, never in a million years." Yes, I can hear it already.* "Nur!" *Now I haven't seen that in quite a while: I thought she'd outgrown that. What is this?* "Oh, Nur, not the carpet!"

She steps out of the kitchen, and with the macaroni and cheese box still firmly in hand, she moves to the edge of the carpet, her toes safely on the kitchen's linoleum, saying, "Nur, enough of this." It is then—the hiss of her "this" still in the air—that he emerges from the garage. *Where'd he go? Found? I'll never get that vomit out, and the smell. . . .* "Saba, where have you been? Do you see your daughter? See what she's done to the carpet? See. . . . You found it?"

The Daughter

Where did that yellow come from? It tastes like eggs. I never eat eggs. But it tastes like eggs. I hope they never find it.

Wednesday's Lunch

Meanwhile, just outside a restaurant, in a hotel, in the middle of the city, a woman is screaming at a policeman to come, motioning with gloved hands for him to hurry. He, leaning up against his police car, cellphone in one hand, cigarette in the other, grudgingly looks up, says good-bye, "I have to go. Yes, yes. I have to go." Straightening his cap, he waits for a break in the traffic before trotting across the street, holding on tight to his black belt that jingles and twinkles with assorted police tools. As he approaches he looks for injury, blood, shattered car parts, but there is nothing, and so, "Yes? What is . . ."

"Arrest him," she says, pointing toward the hotel. "Arrest him now."

Although the policeman is young, he has been on the force for five years and has seen it all: from traffic accidents, hit and runs, heroin, alcohol, to maids leaping from the fifth floor, the sixth floor, the seventh floor, and so on. He waits for her to say more, to get it all out, but surprisingly she has stopped, as if "arrest him" is enough. All this time she hasn't stopped pointing—black-gloved with finger trembling—and he follows her point, realizing that she wants him to look at the window, into the restaurant; and when he does, squinting, he says, "Yes?"

She stamps her foot, repeating, "Arrest him, her, both of them."

Although she is veiled, her eyes are wide and frantic; he puts up one hand to hold back the sun and relooks into the glass. He sees people at tables, some eating—forks moving from food to mouths, bread being buttered, coffee being sipped—some talking, most eating. People in a hotel restaurant. In the end, all he can ask is, "Why?"

She stops in mid-anger to stare at him, and although he can't see her mouth, he can imagine it is opening, closing, fishlike. There is a short silence of only traffic, the roil of city, before her eyes narrow, slit-like, "That's my husband in there, at that table, and he is having lunch, again, with her, his secretary, some Swedish blonde. Now please, do your duty and arrest them. Now. Here."

Once she got the phone call at 11:30, everything, as planned, happened very quickly. She scurried to slip on shoes, spray on perfume, maybe some rouge, brushing her hair with three good strong strokes, and never mind the lipstick, stepping around Wael who had neatly arranged his toys in front of the TV (soldiers on one side, monsters and demons on the other) wanting to know if she will watch cartoons with him, "just for a little while." But side-stepping him, her *abaya* brushing over him like a sail, she yelled, "Maria, I'm going now. I'll be back soon. If anyone comes, calls, tell them I'll be back soon. Wael is here, in front of the TV. Play with him." A "Yes Madam" can be heard from a distant room, followed by another "Yes Madam" and then another until Maria is suddenly there, at the door and slightly out of breath. "Siera, I need the car. Are you ready? The car. Now, Siera." Waiting at the door, tapping her foot, tucking and arranging her *hijab,* now the *niqab,* until all is just right. "Siera?"

Thanks to Siera's driving, knowing all there is to know about shortcuts and slipping in and out of traffic, they arrive quickly.

She, having forgotten her sunglasses and purse but never mind, sitting in the back seat with cellphone at the ready just in case there might be more to know, said, "Pull over here, here, and wait." During the frantic drive from home to hotel, he said nothing, simply nodding at the right time, clicking his tongue to her questions that were not meant for him, but clicking to show that he was on her side.

One hand at his belt, the other at his sunglasses, he waits for a truck to rumble by before, "Madame, I can do nothing. There's nothing wrong here. He has broken no law. No crime."

By now others have stopped to turn and look—a young policeman with a woman. Some never really stop but linger, hover, toying with their cellphones, pretending not to be listening, looking up, then down at their feet, as if their shoes had suddenly become so important. Besides, it is nothing new, an everyday sight: a woman raising her voice, lifting her arms to the sky. Something about husbands and restaurants.

"Law? Don't talk to me about law. You can see for yourself." As if on cue, her husband of eight years leans across the table to point a finger straight into the table cloth, smiling, now laughing, and all the while her blonde head, arching neck, is quivering with laughter until she has to hold a finger against her lips, followed by a long drink of water.

The policeman steps into the shade, hoping she will follow, but she doesn't, won't.

"So you won't help me?"

"Madame . . ."

"You won't help a citizen in need?"

"Madame . . ."

"Yes or no?"

"There is nothing . . ."

"Yes or no?"

When the policeman's cellphone rings he happily moves away to answer it, turning his back on her. But it is nothing, a cousin who wants to talk Manchester United. He says that he must go, that he is busy, that they can talk later, after his shift, *shisha,* and sandwiches. When he turns to start again with her, she is gone. He looks up and down the street, but nothing. Even the onlookers have gone. That's when he looks down and sees a black glove, crimpled, fist-like. He saves looking back into the restaurant window for last, and when he does, husband with Swedish secretary are gone as well. Being a policeman of five years tells him that a missing wife and laughing husband with secretary is not a good combination, and now this glove. He turns and hurries into the restaurant, his police belt with tools clicking, cellphone ringing as he goes.

Just Right

These are the pants that fit just right, that are impossibly tight, designer jeans with red and pink loopy stitching around each and every pocket. And these are the open-toe high heels that if she walks just right—dainty half-steps—will allow her fire-engine red toenails to peek out. This is the blouse that is everything she's ever wanted in a blouse: pirate-like, ruffles, billowing chiffon sleeves. So, she steps to the mirror and slips and pulls and stretches on the jeans, making sure not to look down but straight ahead into the mirror, as if she's watching somebody else do the pulling and buttoning. Finally, with a tiny ring of perspiration around her lips and her jeans in place, she pushes her fingers deep into every pocket to make sure they work. Next is the cream-colored blouse that she bought last summer in Paris, in a shop on the Champs-Élysées. She starts at the bottom buttons and slowly works her way up until there are two buttons left—stopping there—and then she raises her arms to watch the sleeves unfurl and billow. Before the high heels comes the belt, silver and glittery and thick. Still looking into the mirror, she shifts the belt first one way then the other until it softly sags, riding her hips just right. She angles her body right, left, right, left. Finished with this mirror, she steps to the bathroom, shutting, locking the door out of habit.

She is going shopping with Alaya, and their plan, like always, is to have her driver drop them off at the mall, in front, and then the two of them will walk, traveling from shop to shop to shop, fingering clothes, skirts, trying on shoes, spraying on perfume, forever stopping to answer their cellphones and to send a text-message or two, and then—almost done now—stopping for coffee and cake before calling the driver to come around front, to the no-parking zone, to pick them up, taking them home.

But meanwhile and before all that, she is in the bathroom stretching her lips clownlike to get the red of the lipstick on just right. Her bathroom mirrors show all; she stares straight ahead and sees front, back, side, the loopy pinkred of her back pockets, the gunslinger sag of her belt.

She is not married but has plenty of friends who are, some happily, some not, most somewhere in between. She is not in love yet. But if all goes well she will be, and after a couple of years, maybe two at the very most, she will marry. But for now she lives with her family, and everybody, even her father, is happy with that. Later, once she is older and if she stays unmarried, this will change. But no matter, because her father will speak to the mother who will speak to an aunt who knows a second cousin who knows a friend whose son is studying in London, who will be home soon, who . . . For now she has her own room, as it should be.

Leaning over the bathroom sink to get a better look at her face, she applies a collage of powder, cream, something like a rouge. There is a new pimple between her eyes that needs attention; and now that she leans closer, her cheek almost touching the glass, she can see crusty patches of skin behind her ears that require lotioning. A wild hair sticks springlike from one eyebrow. All of this must be fixed. By now she can do it quickly, routinely. Finally, repairs done, she gives her long hair a good brushing, and then a last glance. Standing in front of her mirror that can see anything and everything, she turns, and yes there is no more to do. Besides, she is already late. Alaya is on her way. Quickly she paints her fingernails the same fire-engine red, twittering and fluttering her fingertips like some silly orchestra conductor to help them dry. She dabs on a perfume. Almost done now, saving the best for last.

She paints her eyelids black and green—the colors of coral snakes and frogs—and then uses the tiniest of brushes to tease the eyelashes up and out. Her fingernails all dry now, she hurries to the front door and stops to stare into the mirror that is there. Satisfied, she then slips on the black gloves that are waiting on the tabletop.

With Alaya calling, saying she is in the car waiting, "Hurry up," she aims for the door with Jenny saying, "Oh Madame you look wonderful, beautiful, very beautiful."

"Thank you, Jenny. Thank you."

The black gloves on good and tight, she steps to the coat hooks that are next to the mirror and reaches up to unhook the black *abaya,* slipping it on; and now back to the mirror, looking straight ahead, she takes down the *hijab* and does a quick wrap, and now the *niqab.* In the end, she is ready, her eyes peeking out large and peacock; she is all dressed and ready to go.

Four maybe five hours later she returns. Jenny meets her at the door so she doesn't have to use her key, ring the bell.

"Hello, Madame. You had a good time?"

Stepping inside the house, letting her *niqab* fall away, "Oh, yes, it was wonderful." She holds up two shopping bags to prove it. Moving deeper into the house now, unrolling her *hijab,* shedding the *abaya,* throwing both onto the couch where Jenny, like always, will follow, putting everything back in its rightful place by the door. Once in her room, she shuts the door, locks it out of habit, and goes immediately to the mirror, turning this way and that to see her jeans, high heels, lifting her arms to see the sail of her blouse. When she finishes, she slowly undresses, putting everything back in the closet and drawers just right.

The Border Guard's Philosophy

His small wooden table with its chair are just about perfect for the old bridge. Trucks and cars and buses can squeeze by on the right, people and bicycles on the left. As I approach, I can see that the table's edges are shiny smooth; it has nothing like corners. In the center of the table is an inkpad, beside it a rubber stamp attached to a wooden handle the size of your fist. The tabletop is covered with tiny explosions of purple ink. Because he is busy reading the newspaper, he has not bothered to look up; but certainly he has heard me coming, creaking across the gray planks, and as I step to his table he holds out his one newspaper-free hand and says, "*Awrak'ak*. Papers."

I give him my passport.

He must close his newspaper to do his job, to take my passport.

It is a simple wooden bridge that looks as if it would wrinkle and fold and disappear into the gorge if the right heavy truck came along. He and his table are in the middle of the bridge. Although it is only October, it feels colder, mid-wintry, and so I push my hands deep into my pockets and wait. Because it is not a big noisy river—little more than a creek in places—I can hear the wind blowing through the trees.

His newspaper all closed now, he looks at my passport—not even a look really, more like a glance to see if there is a photograph—and almost immediately says, "*Jayyhit.* Fine," and stamps it with his purple ink.

It is then, as he pushes my passport back across the table to me, that I hear the groaning of that same gray wood I just came across and turn to see an old man stepping onto the bridge. The guard re-opens his newspaper, turning page after page, as if searching for something. I take my passport and blow on the purple ink to dry it off before slipping it back into my jacket. Meanwhile, he has found what he was looking for, smoothing the newspaper flat against the tabletop. I chance a glance, and of course it is football scores. For some reason he has said nothing about my still being there, craning my neck to look over his shoulder, not walking on across the bridge and into another country.

The old man has hold of what looks like a wooden box, but that's not exactly right either, because it has a handle of sorts, not even a handle, really; still, it looks like a wooden box and he's trying to carry it like a suitcase but when that doesn't work he drags it with two hands. I think about giving him a hand, but then thinking again, what if I did? How far do I carry it? Do I carry it across the bridge? To carry his box from there to here, the middle of the bridge, seems almost silly because he has farther to go. And so the old man struggles, scraping closer, and now I can see that his trousers are torn at the knees and especially muddy down one leg. He has a rope for a belt. It isn't long before he and his box arrive at the table and wait for the guard to finish with the football scores. *Salaam Malakum.* Finally, the list of scores all read, he brushes the newspaper off the table, and like a kind of anger the wind immediately yanks it over the edge and into the creek. The guard now holds out his hand and says, "Papers."

Even I can see that this toothless man has nothing like papers—has never had anything like papers—but the guard is strangely patient and continues to hold out his hand. The old man wipes his forehead with what once must have been a white handkerchief, and then smiles, grimaces—who's to know—before saying he needs to get across to see his daughter, his oldest daughter, who he hasn't seen in three, maybe four years; but the bigger more important part of the story is that they, the uncles and aunts, have sent him a message saying she is sick, maybe dying and he needs to see her one last time, so if you don't mind. "You understand, you have a family, too. Yes? Daughters? So you understand."

He is talking to both of us, first looking at me, then him, but both of us just to be sure.

The border guard says nothing, but continues to sit at his table, in the middle of the wooden bridge. The old man can see that this is not good, and so to show him that he is not a smuggler, that he would never think of such a thing, he reaches into his pockets and pulls out an ink pen that looks pale, inkless, along with a ragged pack of cigarettes. "See, nothing."

By now the guard is running his thumbnail along the edge of the table, saying again, "Papers."

With this the old man knows what is what, and so he picks up his wooden box that is wrapped in rope and knotted at the top in something like a handle and slowly heads back across the bridge. When he comes to the end of the bridge and moves off the dirt road and onto a path, he stumbles, rights himself, stumbles again, and with a kind of elegance collapses under the trees. As I watch him stretched out next to his box, a courage wells up in me and just like that I turn to the guard, who is now looking closely at his thumb, and ask, "Why can't you let him cross? He is an old man, harmless. He only wishes to see his daughter, nothing more. An old man. Why not? Who cares?"

My voice startles him, as if he has forgotten I am still there. He looks one last time at his thumb, and now smiling, says, "Papers. He must have papers. It's the law, you know."

That's when a breeze comes up, and because it feels especially cool and fresh, neither of us says anything until it is done, and when it is, I ask, "What will he do, this old man?" It is not a good question, and I am not even sure what I mean. And yet, I say it again, "What will he do?"

The border guard has a moustache that is wiry bushy, and I can see where he has tried waxing it smooth but it hasn't worked. His uniform is the color of green dusty olives.

He shrugs and says, "He will cross the creek down there," motioning with his chin. "Down there by the two boulders, that's the shallow part. They cross down there."

I wait for more, but there is nothing; he goes back to his thumb. He leaves me little choice but to say, "But if you know this, why not stop them—these people crossing illegally? I mean, you just said it's your job. They need papers to cross."

He sharply gives up on his thumb and for the first time squints at me, searching my face. Slowly, as if I am a child and he wants me to understand each and every word, he says, "At night I can see them crossing, their lanterns bobbing. But my job is this bridge. We don't want smugglers using the bridge, crossing illegally on this bridge. This is against the law. I stop them from smuggling, from sneaking across the bridge. That is my job."

"Yes," my face is hot from being spoken to like a child, "but as you say, they are breaking the law. If you see them crossing there, what is the difference: here, there? What?"

On the front of his cap is what once must have been a bright silver buckle, with a number, but now it is tarnished and unreadable.

He removes the cap. Like his moustache, his hair is bushy and wild and sadly comic, and he sighs like he is getting ready to tell a story that he has told many times before and, quite frankly, is tired of telling, but one last time, and so, "Right this moment, as we speak on this bridge, people are breaking the law in New York City. I know this. They are robbing people in Paris, murdering in Hamburg, raping in London. In China, crime is everywhere, all day, every day. I have not been to these places but I know this to be true. And so, the very best I can do," looking down at his dusty boots on this wooden bridge, "is to not let them break the law here, across my bridge. This is my job, you see. I am but one man, and this is my bridge, my table. This one bridge is my responsibility. Surely as an American you can understand this."

When I lean to see his face, to get a better look at what he means, suddenly the rubber stamp requires a close inspection and he takes it in both hands.

Later that evening and just across the border, as I am getting ready for sleep in something like a small hotel that charges far too much, I can't help but hear a familiar scraping moving along the street and now turning down an alleyway, and when I go to the window to see, of course it is the old man with his wooden box, his pants doubly dark, glistening, still wet.

The Ballad of Fat Ali

Ali is fat. His mom blames it on big bones. "The boy is big boned. I am the same, as was my mother and her mother. Big boned people run in the family. What's to be done?" Looking to the heavens. His dad says Ali is big for his age. "Ali is just big for his age, that's all. It happens all the time. It's a new generation, look around."

When Ali plays football there is an unspoken boy's understanding that he will be the last one chosen, that he will play goalie, that if his team loses it will be his fault. Ali would rather not be fat, if you ask him. "I'd rather not be fat." In fact, he'd rather be anything else but fat. "If you gave me choices I'd rather have a rash, be bald, have worms, anything but fat." Shrugging. "But . . ."

There you have it.

Ali smokes but his heart isn't in it. His friends tell him not to worry about the smoking part. "You don't smoke that much, not like the rest of us, so don't worry about it." Ali nods when he hears this. In the beginning, Ali's mother cried when she found a pack of cigarettes in his room, in his closet, behind his shirts. The father shook his head when he heard the news. The wife looking at him, unsure if the shaking meant this or that.

Ali insists that he does not eat that much. "I don't eat that much. Not really." His uncle on his mother's side, who is also fat, says it has to do with genetics. "It's in the family, and not only that, it has to do with metabolism. Everybody knows that." Ali's uncle did graduate studies in the USA, at the University of Michigan, so he knows what he's talking about. Ali likes his uncle's answers, especially the metabolism part, and uses it whenever he can. "It's not my fault, it's somewhere in here," pointing to his chest, "my metabolism, deep down in my metabolism."

Ali almost always wears a *dishdasha.* Life is easier in so many ways when you can tent yourself in white, or gray, sometimes brown.

But there is more to Ali than fat and smoke and *dishdashas,* he sweats too much. And when he sweats too much he is unpleasant to be around, there is a big wetness, an odor. Nobody is sure if Ali knows about the odor part. His uncle has never mentioned it, not once; his friends have joked about it but with friends and jokes it's hard to tell truth from fiction. Still, if he had to choose, Ali would rather sweat a lot than be fat. "I'd rather sweat all day and all night than be fat. I'd rather stink of sweat than be fat." He takes a puff of his cigarette, blowing smoke straight up into the air.

Once, Ali's mother—his father too busy working at the ministry—took him to the doctor about his weight. When the German-trained doctor walked into the examination room and saw Ali, his mother sitting next to him on one of those silver stools, he said, "It would be good if you lost weight."

Ali, who was taught to respect his elders, especially grandparents and teachers and assorted doctors, could not help but feel angry, annoyed, and found himself saying, "But you don't know why I'm here." His mother tried to shush him but of course it was too late. The German-trained doctor, shrugged, "It's a first impression. So, why are you here?"

Ali told him, "They tell me I am overweight. Some say fat, but I don't think so. Fat is different than overweight, don't you think? Besides, it's all a matter of genes and metabolism. Right? Especially the metabolism."

The German-trained doctor placed Ali's chart on the table, took off his glasses and looked long and hard and doctorly at the boy and his mother. Fingering Ali's chart, he said, "Ali, is it?"

"Yes."

"Ali, you are fat."

Ali did not like this. His mother stopped smiling, her hands tight in her lap.

"You need to lose weight."

Ali looked down at his hands, and said, "How much?"

The German-trained doctor frowned and said, "Fifteen, sixteen kilos would be nice."

"That much?" said Ali's mother.

"That much?" said Ali.

The German-trained doctor said it again, "Fifteen kilos for starters."

Mother with Ali rose from their silver stools to leave, but as they moved to the door, the German-trained doctor asked them if they knew what diabetes was? "Do you know what diabetes is?"

Both of them said yes, although neither was really sure. Something about blood and sugar.

In the end, Ali and his mother half-heartedly thanked the doctor and went home. Ali drove because his mother was too busy being worried, her hands knotted white in her lap.

Ali thought losing weight would not be difficult. One kilo here, another there, and after two weeks or so, a lighter Ali would appear. In the meantime, Ali had malls to visit, friends to sit with, *shishas* to smoke, text messages to send. Not only that, but right across the street is a *bakala*. Ali can see it from his bedroom window.

Over the weeks, Ali tried to lose weight, but the more he tried the harder it became. His shoes hurt his feet, his stomach whined in the middle of the night. One morning he woke up with dandruff. Finally, after four weeks and two days of not losing weight, Ali ran away.

It was not a big running away, just two days, but long enough for his mother not to know where he was, to call the police two, three times, to stay up all night worrying that her son was dead in a ditch somewhere. Ali's father canceled his *diwaniya*.

When Ali returned two days later, around lunchtime, his mother rushed to hug and kiss him, asking him where he had been. "Where in God's name have you been?" The father, waking up from his nap, stepped into the room, rubbing his eyes, roaring, "You had your mother worried to death."

Ali said he was sorry. "I'm sorry."

"Well sorry isn't enough, now is it?"

Ali, having not forgotten to respect his elders, parents, and assorted doctors, said, "No, sir, I suppose not."

Ali had been at his friend's chalet, with computer games, a pool table. This is the part he didn't say.

But in the end all was forgotten because after all, their son was back.

Ali wasn't exactly sure how his being fat and his running away were related, just that they were, in some way. But no matter, to celebrate Ali's return his mother—all done being sad and without her only son—cooked a big meal, Ali's favorite, spaghetti and meatballs.

The Sweet Cart Papers

In the middle of the mall, wedged neatly in between gurgling fountain and escalator, is something like a cart, except bigger. It has large wooden, wagon-like wheels that don't turn—have never turned. That, and it's piled high with plastic containers that are full of many-colored candies, chocolates, and licorices. This, the sign says, is the Sweet Cart.

I watch two *dishdashas* with sunglasses take seats at the next door coffee shop, and almost immediately the one raises his hand like some school boy to get the waiter's attention, and of course the waiter, William, who is from Cebu, whose uncle knows my uncle, comes and even before he has a chance to say "Sir, Yes Sir," he is told that they need an ashtray—finger tapping the tabletop—and that the table and chairs behind them are too close, they can't stretch their legs, and that. . . . Just as William is getting ready to look this way, I quickly turn to the nearest container, chocolate balls, and taking the tiny plastic shovel give them a good stir.

At one end of the mall is Simon who is in charge of the brightly-colored kiddy carts. Simon is 35, maybe 36, and his job is to make sure that the kids get the right color cart, with the right number. He tells me that the blue 99 is popular. On a busy Friday or Saturday, you can see his kiddy carts being driven all over the mall, little drivers running over potted plants, nipping heels. He sometimes waves to me from his end of the mall, like we are on different islands and the sea is deep and dark between us, waving both arms like he needs rescuing.

Which reminds me of the time during Ramadan when an old man fell, right over there next to the bakery, and he couldn't get up. People slowed to look, a small circle of men and women forming around him, looking, motioning for him to get up, "What's the matter with you?" Finally, Simon, seeing what was what, deserted his kiddy cart post and rushed to the closet where they keep things like mops, buckets, wheelchairs, crutches, . . . and pulled the wheelchair out, knocking down the crutches with a clatter, and rushed to the fallen man, who, by now, was leaning on one elbow looking up, talking. Simon is good like that: helping old fallen men when others are too busy asking them what's the matter. He didn't have to, Simon; his job is to keep the brightly-colored kiddy carts clean, ready, and in a neat little row underneath the escalator.

I can't give out Sweet Cart samples, no matter who they say they are or who they know. Mr. Prem is very firm on this point. Sometimes Mr. Prem comes by and asks, "How's it going?" And like always, I say Good or Fair or Fine or OK, and he replies, Good, Fine, or OK, and maybe stays long enough to take a handful of his favorite, Cola Worms. Mr. Prem, my boss.

Just this morning two boys with nanny come running up, one going that way, the other this, and all the while their nanny is telling them to wait, wait. But the bigger one can't be bothered with nannies, and sticks his hand in the green mints, stuffing them into his mouth. This, he thinks, is funny, laughing chocolaty, green teeth. And now the smaller one, with tennis shoes that flash red with every step, takes a fistful of Gummy Bears, and fits them neatly into his mouth. Although I'm there at his side, hands behind my back, he thinks nothing of plunging his tiny hand in again—deeper, Gummi Bears clinging to the plastic edge, tumbling onto the floor. By now the nanny has caught up to them and is pulling at their shirts, saying Sorry and No, no, and Sorry. But tugging at their shirts only makes for more fun. That's when I see the mother standing by the fountain with cellphone against her ear, smiling, shaking her head as if to say isn't that something, those boys, aren't they something?

And then there was February, during Valentine's Day, the young woman who said she needed 300 grams of anything, "You decide, anything, but hurry, 300 grams." So I went from container to container, shoveling in some of this, a little of that. In the end, the woman, who had never stopped looking down at her cellphone, pushing numbers and smiling, more numbers and smiling some more, and now, finally, talking to a Mohammed, or Hamad, or Ed, who was very funny because she couldn't stop laughing, took the bag of many-colored candy, pushed a five dinar bill into my hand, and hurried away. I called out to her once, twice, "Change, Madam, your change," but she never looked back, not once, she was too busy laughing at Mohammed, Hamad, or Ed.

Or, how about yesterday, the fellow with the blue suit and matching blue tie who looked like he knew all there was to know about having money, about being an executive, who walked up, hands behind his back, looking, deciding, until he stopped in front of the chocolate malt balls, saying, "Gimme those."

"Yes."

"What?" His hands slowly coming undone from behind his back. "What?"

"Yes."

"Yes sir, You mean yes sir."

"Yes sir."

His blue arms making a perfect X across his blue tie, and he said, "Don't they train you to be polite here?"

"Yes sir," hurrying to fill the bag with chocolate malt balls. "How much, sir?"

"Now it's sir?"

"Yes sir."

"Now it's sir."

"How many grams, sir?"

"What's your name?"

I pointed to my nametag. "Sally, sir."

In the coffee shop William was busy wiping tables, lifting ash-trays and napkins and knives and forks and wiping tables. He, of course, heard all, but refused to look up.

Reaching deep into his blue coat pocket, he took out a golden pen followed by a small packet of paper and wrote my name—Sally. When he finished I held out his bag of chocolate malt balls, and he snatched it, saying, "I know your boss, Sally. I know him well, and he'll hear about this. You'll see."

It was only later, as I watched him walk blue-suited pass the fountain, up the escalator and out the door—William finally glancing over at me—that I remember he didn't pay.

Payday is in two days. Last month they were late five days, the month before that, two weeks. It's not their fault, they say. Mr. Prem says, "It's not my fault," motioning with palms up. I tell Mr. Prem about the man in the blue suit who didn't pay, who said he knew him, who said he would report me for not sirring him. Mr. Prem says he doesn't know anybody with blue suits and blue ties, and when he asks me to describe him, I say he wasn't very tall and wore sunglasses and had a black beard, and, "Oh yes, his English was off."

"Off?"

"Off."

He still doesn't know him, has never heard of a blue-suited man with off English. Finally, he says I will have to pay for what he stole. He will take it out of my salary. "It's only fair, right?" Mr. Prem, my boss in charge of the Sweet Cart.

Right after that I look down the mall and Simon is standing there looking my way, and when he sees me, he, like always, waves his arms.

Tiny brown birds fly inside the mall, flickering from one fake palm to the next. Nobody knows how they got there, one day they just showed up. Sometimes in the evening, when the mall is closing and it's just me, the others, and security, the birds swoop down to the fountain to bathe and sneak a drink. It doesn't bother them if I walk right up to the water's edge and sit down. In fact, it's almost as if they don't even know I'm there.

Another Country's Waitress

I sit down at the small wooden table against the wall, next to the window, and wait for her to come over. The walls groan and sigh as the wind and sand peck at the glass. A line of candy-colored flower pots hangs from the wall; they quiver. It has been blowing hard all day and all night. The next time I look up, there she is. Softly, silently, she slips a menu into my hand—a hand that is still dusty and unready for anything like a menu. Her arms are lean and brown. I look up into her face but she is looking the other way—a black ringlet swirling over her ear. I stretch to see what she sees but there is only the sand and wind at the window.

"Do you remember me?" I smile.

She smiles a smile that looks tired, practiced. "Of course. You are here two, maybe three days past. That table there." Motioning toward a table next to the flowerpots. "I remember you. I remember all of you."

The wind tugs at the window, and the shop moans. Nodding, I pick up the menu and give it back to her. "Just coffee."

"Yes." And she steps away.

She slips behind the counter and goes through the slow perfect ritual of making coffee. When done, she pours it into a small white cup and brings it to me—the tiniest of clicks as porcelain meets wood. I look out the window and see palm fronds swaying, shaking. Leaves tumble and whirl. There is music—guitars, piano, and more—but the sand storm is too big to hear all of it.

"You don't look so happy. What happened—lose a boyfriend?"

It's an unfunny joke, and I must know it because I say it to the coffee, its steam spinning into my eyes.

"No," she whispers. "That's not it."

That's when I look into her face. It isn't a waitress's face, not at all; it's young and strangely soft around the eyes and chin. A wisp of hair at her temple.

"But something?"

"Nothing so big."

Thinking that all is done, that there is nothing left to say, I take a sip of too-hot coffee, waiting for her to move away, to go back to work behind the counter. But she doesn't move—standing there, rubbing her childlike fingers along the table's edge.

"It must be a secret then."

"No, not a secret." And she tries another smile.

The storm roars, and now something tumbles past the window, brushing and thumping as it goes. Swaying flowerpots, and a windy rippling across the ceiling. Her lips move as if she is trying to remember a word.

"A boyfriend?" I guess.

"Yes," watching her fingers rub the smooth wood. "That's it."

Putting both my hands around the white coffee cup.

She turns to look about the shop, her ringlet bouncing—the clean curve of her throat. The floor is old and brown, and when the light hits it just right I can see where it dips and dimples.

"He has two girlfriends, you see—me and another."

I wait for more but she has stopped to watch her fingers rub the wood. Taking my hands away from the coffee cup, I say, "That doesn't sound so bad."

"No, but . . ." Her fingers done rubbing now, and she looks at my face, then at my hands, and now at my face again. "No, but we did sex, you see. Intercourse."

The guitars get louder and the wind comes faster, harder, drowning out the piano, and I can feel the redness on my neck, around my ears.

"Yes, and he have another girlfriend, and now I don't know what should I do."

When I look up at her, there is just the calm of her face and the straight-white of her teeth. I expect something more, something bigger. I sip. Even though I don't want to, I sip.

"Are you in trouble?"

"In trouble?"

Sipping some more, not tasting the coffee now. "Yes, you know, trouble?" Making a tumbling motion with my hand to help show her what trouble looks like.

"Oh no," her white teeth showing something like a real smile. "Nothing like that."

"That's good. That's something."

"Yes, something, but he have another girlfriend and he tells her about us, everything, and now I think she must be sad too."

After that we are quiet for a while. Her fingers go back to stroking the tired wood. My coffee is almost gone. The sand and wind twisting and pulling at the window, and then there is a whistling—a kettle-whistling.

"He likes us both. This is what he tells me."

"And you believe him?"

She frowns, her slender fingers stopping. "I don't know." Still frowning, her tongue glistening over her lips.

It is then that the door is flung open and three men shuffle into the shop. Napkins flutter and potted plants teeter, as a piece of the storm follows the men in. They all wear sunglasses even though there has been no sun all day. One of them has a moustache, the other two are wearing slickers that are dull and brown with sand. They slowly take them off, hang them up, sit at the counter. She hurries over to them.

I finish my coffee and listen to the three men talk about how it has been blowing all day. Driving is impossible. She is busy doing something behind the counter. Although it doesn't look to be important, she is doing it anyway.

Finally there is nothing left to do but pay for the coffee and leave. I slip on my coat and hat and step to the counter. As she takes my money, her eyes move to the three men. The one with the moustache is talking about dust clouds, the shape and color of dust clouds. Another says it never used to be so bad, so thick and day after day after day, but ever since the war and the Americans with their tanks and heavy equipment, they've churned up the desert, and this is what they get, motioning toward the door. Their sunglasses neatly folded in front of them, on the countertop.

When she gives me the change, her hand lingers, her fingertips resting on the coins. She is looking at my chin, maybe even my throat. With the man still talking about dust clouds, she whispers, "Must I leave him?"

Because I am a foreigner, an American, and because I hardly know her, I say, "Yes. Absolutely."

The Jungles of Basra

Her name is Nasreen, but she will answer to Nancy. In fact, only her Arabic friends call her Nancy, everybody else calls her Nasreen.

"It's kinda funny, don't you think? Even ironic. Is that the word?"

Although her hair is long, black, secretly he thinks there is no such thing as pure black hair; there is always that tinge of brown, that aura of henna when the sunlight hits it just right. But Nasreen is different; her hair is black. He's tried her from different angles, standing so the biggest and brightest window is behind her, catching her in its autumn yellow, watching intently as she brushes strands away from her cheeks; it squirrels around her neck, and every time, it is black—a nighttime jungle black. It flows pass the thin curve of her shoulder blades, not even bones, more like wings of flesh peek-a-booing through the glistening blackness.

It is the third class, maybe the fourth, but on a Thursday for sure; and once everyone has gone, it is just the two of them because she stays behind, pretending to be looking for something in her bag, something that refuses to be found. Finally giving up her search, she looks up and is softly surprised to see him still there, but since he is she says, "Do you know Basra?"

"Yes."

"My home, my village, is up north," pointing up, "in the desert, not far from Basra."

He nods.

On this day, the Thursday of her telling him that she is from Iraq, she has done something with her hair that he has never seen before. She put it up and over in something like a fold in the back; it glistens doubly, and when he looks for some kind of band or pin holding it all together, he sees none.

"Sometimes I am homesick, you know. Homesick. Yes, of course I like this place," using both hands to show him this place and how she likes it. "But it's not the same."

"What is the name of your home, your village?"

This surprises her, and her eyes grow big, bigger, and she stops to think, tilting her head puppy-like.

"It's a small, unimportant village. You would not know it. Nobody knows it except those who live there. It doesn't matter. Just some village in the middle of the desert, with a river over there, some train tracks over here, Basra, 150, maybe 160 kilometers that way." Pointing through the window, into the brightness of September.

That night he has a dream, and it is green and hot and somewhere faraway. A wet heat with blueblack jungle and wrist-thick vines. He turns in his sleep, even slides his hands under the pillow to look for cool, but the hot follows him everywhere. When he wakes it feels like a short dream but he is sweating, his hair is wet, shower-like; he is exhausted. Looking at the clock and forgetting it is Friday, he sees, like always, that it is time to get up. He can't help but feel a good weakness, like after a sickness—all used up and thinner, lighter, and wonderfully empty.

That first dream of jungle follows him all that day and into the next. It's like no dream he's ever had; the others were almost always fresh and clear in the morning, and he could remember everything about them as he stood in the shower, the hot water pelting his face; but as the mornings wore on these other dreams grew weak, weaker, faded, until finally nothing by afternoon. But this jungle dream is different, growing bigger, and he sometimes remembers something brand new about it in the middle of the day: the way a fistful of bright yellow birds flickered in and out of the creepers, the jungle holding them like a second night. By Sunday afternoon, new and exciting details continue to fall into place.

He really shouldn't be thinking things like that in the middle of the day, not when students are lined up at the door, sitting on the floor, clustered around the podium, because they need to take his course to graduate, to get their degree, to get jobs, to make money, to . . . Still, he steps to the window and lets them wait. There is a mumbling, heads turning to see the big clock on the wall behind them, faces staring down into their cellphones. But he continues looking out the window, into the dusty trees, seeing nothing like yellow birds. The windows on the third floor are fine squares of glass that are not meant to be opened because this building has central air and why would anyone need to open a window. Finally he sees a small unimportant brown bird fly to the ledge. It hops, maybe twitters, and then, done with both, blurs away. In the end, he has looked far too long and they are restless and so he turns and goes to the board and writes his name and talks about things that all teachers talk about the very first day of class. He gives them copies of a syllabus that is filled with directions and guidelines and rules. They secretly like this. He neglects talking about grades, but toward the end they can't help but demand more information about numbers and letters. Some backward-capped young man asks, "How long do these papers have to be?" He tells them not to worry—later, but not the first day of class. They do not like answers like this, he can tell. A shuffling of feet, heads craning to see how much time is left. Two cellphones go beep, buzz, and each time he waits until their alarms stop.

In the morning he almost always has a cup of coffee and jam on toast. Later, sometimes when he is thinking of other things—aiming his head up and to the right, as if there is something to be read in that corner of the ceiling—he can't remember what he had for breakfast, or even if he ate at all, but he must have and it must have been coffee, toast with jam, because that is what he always has. For lunch he has a sandwich, salami and cheese, ice water; for dinner, another sandwich, less cheese, more salami. Of course she cooks and there are other foods, but later, perhaps when they are asleep, he will move through the house, down the stairs, and have his sandwich.

Wednesday mornings are extra quiet because the daughters go to school, she to work, and he has no classes until mid-morning. Sipping coffee while looking at the dog look back at him through the screen door, he lets its steam work on his face and thinks of Nasreen, her hair, and then—the dog scratching at the screen, now jumping, showing the pink of its belly—remembering the day the second daughter was born, how the same dog, smaller, pinker, scratched at that same screen, whining, when somebody's cousin, maybe nephew, said, "Another girl? Too bad, hey?" All the while shaking his hand, grinning.

Nasreen raises her hand while others blurt out answers, half answers, thinking this is the stuff of learning. All the while her hand remains straight, tall, waiting to be called upon no matter what. He calls on her and she does her best to explain. When she stops to fumble over the right word, two others jump in to fill the quiet, but when he holds up his hand like some traffic cop they stop; meanwhile, Nasreen has found the right word, and it is *regardless*. When class is finished, she is the last to leave, the only one to wave good-bye. He finds himself waving back.

The next dream is of a grove in that same jungle. It is mist-filled, followed by the double black of the jungle and then an evening sky bristling with stars and planets. The moment the dream starts, his sweat begins, the damp hollow of the pillow, but like before he feels good and used up, and when a breeze finds its way through the trees, it makes everything extra cool, even cold. Like all dreams, he has no idea why he is there in the jungle, how he arrived; there is a hum in the trees. In this dream, it is understood that he is to wait, to sweat, and to watch the mist swirl. The humming throbs like a pulse while the mist grows thin, thinner, gone.

"What's the matter?"

"What?"

"Are you sick?"

"Sick?"

"You're soaked. Fever? Cold? What?"

"No, maybe it's the blankets."

"The blankets?"

She yawns, stretches and moves toward the bathroom. He runs his hand through his wet sticky hair. He never thought of it as sickness, not once.

Yousef is forever angry. He frowns at any and all homework assignments.

"How are you today, Yousef?"

"Tired."

"Impossible, you're too young to be tired."

Yousef has pimples and something wrong with his earlobes; they are impossibly broken, sticking out like wings. When he frowns he looks like someone from one of those wanted posters. He has to turn away when Yousef decides to frown because if Yousef sees him smirking, it will only make things worse. Yousef sits in the back, under the clock, and has long dark hair that he keeps in a tight, slick ponytail.

"You stayed up too late, heh?"

"Maybe."

Yousef is older than the others, maybe thirty. So, his questions are often tough and double-daring: "How do you know?" "Why is that important?" "Will that be on the test?" Yousef is the only one who knows what the word *crenellate* means.

Nasreen wears a necklace that is more red string and jade than necklace. At first he thinks it is an animal—dragon, lion, some kind of horse—but after two weeks of looking when she isn't, he's convinced it's nothing more than a block of jade. She wears it so tight against her throat that it wobbles when she talks.

In the back, not far from Yousef, sit the lovers, their chairs angled so the edges touch. Almost always they are smiling at each other. He doesn't mind them because they are in the back, say little and care nothing about the class. In fact, he envies them; if envy is not the right word, then jealousy is. He wears a baseball cap; she keeps her hair in braids every day, different ribbons, same braids. Although they are both failing the course, they have no cellphones; they spend fifty minutes looking at one another, whispering. He can't be angry with them.

In front and to the right of the lovers sits Bedour. When called upon she painfully squeezes out the biggest, best answers. Bedour has never once felt the need to raise her hand. He must wait for her to lift her eyes from the book before, "And Bedour, what do you think?" He knows all about Bedour. High school teachers have told her that her writing is wonderful, unique, correct, that she has a way with words, and, oh, by the way, has she ever thought about going into journalism? So yes, he knows Bedour. She doesn't watch TV, but reads; in fact, reading is like a drug to her, without her daily read she feels terrible, rotten, her day is ruined. Why go out with friends when she can stay home and read about love and death and hate and more love. Anything less than a grade of A and she pouts.

With Ramadan not more than a week away, Nasreen is waiting for him when he walks in early, and although she says good morning, he can tell it's the fluff of unimportant talk. What she really means is that she can't read his writing, holding up her paper alongside her head. He puts down his briefcase and says good morning back, but she is not looking at him, only her paper. He squints at the pages, following the aim of her finger, and says the word is "very." She looks closer at the very. By now he knows Nasreen, and she cares nothing about the word very; he waits for the other, the rest, the bigger, more important questions. Finally, "This grade is no good."

Together, they look at the letter D she is pointing to.

"Yes, you're right."

Her finger refuses to leave the paper, the D. "This is not right."

He waits.

"I mean, this grade is not right."

Still, waiting, watching her finger, her well-chewed fingernails.

"You grade too hard."

"Think so?"

"Of course. Everybody says so. So hard, so unfair."

By now others have started to come in, sitting here, standing there, making that last minute cellphone call because for the next fifty minutes they will be out of touch.

"For example?"

She sighs, letting him know she cares nothing for examples. "For example, here. What is this?"

"That's what we call a run-on sentence. You may recall we talked about that last week, and the week before that, and . . ."

"OK, it's a run-on sentence, but you can still understand my feelings, can't you?"

"Yes I can."

"Then what's so bad? Understanding is most important, right?"

"Yes, that's part of it."

His yes seems to help and she edges closer, her shoulder brushing his, her hair leaning across his arm. More students fill the room. Some of them have decided to listen, as if his answers may in some way be of use to them later on.

"Nasreen, class is about to begin. We'll talk more after class."

She pulls her finger away from the run-on sentence.

Nasreen has new jewelry, rings on her thumbs, one a kind of wrap-a-round silver, the other, a glistening gold.

For the first time, Nasreen does not linger after class; she does not stop to dig through her bag to find that elusive something; she does not wave good-bye at the door. She leaves with the others.

That evening his daughters squabble over sweaters. Although he spends the evening aimed at the TV, he hears everything they say. He dreams of rotting palm fronds bunched snake-like around the trees, the sweet stench of decay wafting across the jungle floor. As he sits on a rock that has a thin fur of moss on one side, the odor climbs off the ground and like a thing with legs, quickly finds his feet, his thighs, trickling across his chest and into his face, nose, bringing tears to his eyes. He shakes his head and shuffles his feet but a smell like this will not be denied, worming up through the leaves and vines and black earth, filling the long fingers of sunlight.

In the morning, he wakes to voices still arguing over clothes, this time shoes.

Nasreen has cut her hair. That, and she no longer sits up front but has taken a seat in the back, two seats from Yousef. When Yousef leans to say something to her, she nods, smiles, and touches the tips of her new hair.

He talks about their final paper, a research paper, due in two weeks, and almost immediately Yousef raises his hand, saying, "Why?"

"Why?"

"Yeah, why do we have to do a research paper?" Folding his arms across his chest. "I mean, how useful will writing a research paper ever be for us, any of us?"

He shrugs.

Even the lovers take time out to listen, looking first at Yousef, then him, now back to Yousef. Nasreen hasn't stopped fingering her new hair.

He readies himself to say something long and complicated, but then, at the last moment, changes his mind and says, "It will be good for you."

Bedour looks straight at him. The lovers twitter.

"That's it?" says Yousef.

"That's it."

He can tell that Yousef is disappointed. Bedour goes back to looking down at her desktop; the lovers go back to each other.

Somebody, somewhere snickers. When he looks at Nasreen she is looking at Yousef.

Mohamed comes to him on a Wednesday, and asks if there is anything he can do.

"Do?"

"Yes, to improve my grade?"

"You're not doing well?"

"No."

The silence of a classroom on a Thursday before Ramadan. Moving a stack of papers from here to there, slipping a book into his briefcase, he looks into Mohamed's face, a face that doesn't want to look back, that almost certainly would rather be looking anywhere else but at him.

"If I don't pass, my dad will be furious."

This is the longest, most complicated sentence Mohamed has ever spoken to him.

"I see."

"You know how it is."

"How's that?"

"It's an Arabic thing, this good grade stuff."

More nodding.

"Is there something I can do, like extra credit?"

"Extra credit?"

"Sure, something like that."

"I don't have anything like that."

Mohamed slanting in front of him, saying nothing and then nodding as if he has heard wisdom.

Nasreen doesn't come to class the Thursday after her new short hair; it is the first time she has missed all term. Without her the class drones. He reminds them about how examples and details are important to any writing, going to the board and giving them examples of examples. They look at him but even he can tell that they are not hearing, seeing.

The term is coming to an end, and Nasreen hasn't stopped sitting in the back, between Mohamed and Yousef. She spends much of the class looking at her hands, her new jewelry. Her black hair is slowly growing back. Another Thursday, and he lets them leave early, and they are happy, even thankful. One of them comes up to him and says, "Thank you." He does not know how to take this, and simply says, "You're welcome." Only Bedour looks worried. Before Nasreen has a chance to leave, he places himself near her, under the clock, and as the others shuffle out, he asks how she is. She answers in a whisper, "Fine." It is the sort of one word answer that is meant to appease, to halt all further questions. As she turns to leave, he notices that she is without her necklace, the red string, the piece of jade.

After Nasreen, his jungle dreams slowly disappear. He has one last sweaty visit in December. The creepers take on a life of their own, magically snaking down and around to grab his arms, squeezing his legs; they slither noose-like around his neck. He wakes sputtering, coughing. She mutters what sounds like a question. When he peers out the window, there is the blush of daylight.

When he walks out on the porch, the dog looks up at him, whimpering because he wants to play, be fed, both, but sitting there at his feet looking up. He doesn't look down at it, but with arms folded studies the way the clouds are mushroom rosy. For what feels like a long time, he stands out on the porch with the dog and thinks of things like sentence fragments and thesis statements and comma splices and D papers. All of this moves smoothly between brightening sky and moaning dog.

The new spring term has started, and after the first class she comes up to him and says she isn't registered for the class and she knows he said there were no more seats available but she would really like to join his class if that is at all possible and even if there isn't enough room she doesn't mind sitting on the floor, if that's ok with him, and. . . . Her piece of jade is bigger, greener, her hair wispy, nothing like Nasreen's. Now she is done talking and is waiting, and since he hasn't said a thing she looks down, thinking that silence must be the same as no. But he is looking at her greenbrown shard of jade, the way it is caught in the scoop of her throat, lazing there on its side, resting. He takes out his pen. "What is your name?"

She is smiling now, small white teeth. "My name is Noura, and . . ."

At Poolside

There are three of them, with sunglasses, under one of the hotel's biggest, bluest umbrellas, when she comes through the door and into the bright sunlight. Their packs of cigarettes, cellphones, and lighters are in neat little piles on the tabletop in front of them. One picks up his lighter and toys with it, another stares into his cellphone, the other, arms neatly folded across his chest, watches her. With her towel draped over one shoulder, she must walk right in front of them to get to the pool. The one refolds his arms and watches her approach, thinking, *Haram*.

As she gets closer, bare shouldered, long-legged, not caring anything about it being Ramadan, this time he says for all to hear, "*Haram*." The others look at him then at the blonde, who by now has gone to the nearest lounge chair, slipped off her watch and shoes, and stepped into the pool. They watch her as she sits on the pool steps—half in half out of the water.

Two of them have beards, the third a moustache that really doesn't look like a moustache, more like he was in a hurry and just taped something black under his nose. He yawns and reaches for what should have been a cup of coffee, a bottle of water, perhaps a glass of juice, but of course there is nothing but a silver ashtray, a silver ashtray that he turns this way and that, and then picks up to look at the bottom. The other two watch him, as if he has found a sign, a message, and now is the time for him to read it. Done looking, squinting, he pushes the ashtray back toward the center of the table. That done, they look at their watches.

A fourth will come later. In fact, he's calling now to say he'll be there shortly. "*Inshallah.*" When the one can't help but ask how much later, he says, "Thirty minutes at the most, maybe forty. Forty minutes."

"OK," he says. "Family, is it?"

"Yes, of course, forty, forty-five minutes."

Finally, the one with the biggest brightest lighter grabs his pile of cigarettes, lighter, and cellphone, pushes back his chair, and announces, "I'll be right back." He walks around the corner and through a door that leads to other doors that lead to the basement, roof, back alley.

On the other side of the pool is a gang of umbrellas tightly bound to their poles. Tiny brown birds swoop down to the deep, shadowy end of the pool; they hop to the water's edge to drink, to see what bugs might be floating by. All done now, they flutter away to lean magically sideways on the trunks of nearby palms. When he returns he sits and says nothing, but after awhile begins to hum.

The other has uncrossed his arms long enough to take off his sunglasses, give his eyes a good rub, and then quickly slip them back on again. He lifts his cigarette lighter from the pile and taps it on the tabletop. Meanwhile, the sun is wedged perfectly between two buildings, its last sunlight blaring into his face. "Somebody should tell her it's Ramadan. That's the hotel's job, isn't it? Somebody needs to tell her what part of the world she's in. This isn't Barcelona, Laguna Beach. Somebody needs to tell her."

Tapping his cigarette lighter and nodding.

"What's the time for today?"

"Time?"

"For *Iftar,* the time?" Done tapping.

“Yesterday was 5:33, so today must be 5:31, something like that.”

They watch her swim, long blonde strokes. She is the only one in the pool, going back and forth.

“How many is that?”

“What?”

“How many laps has she done?”

A helicopter appears over the rooftop, slanting toward the city. Even though they are wearing sunglasses, they shade their eyes to look. “Somebody’s sheikh,” he says.

“Six, seven?”

This time the one with the cellphone that winks blue and red stands up, grabs his pile of cigarettes and lighter, stretches like it is early morning, and says, “Be right back.” They watch him go as if his walking away is important and they need to watch him as long and as hard as they can. Once he steps around the corner, both of them, as if rehearsed, look down at their watches.

She is all done with her laps now, bobbing in the deep shadowy end. She is looking straight up into the sky, and when they follow her gaze they see another helicopter. They wait for it to move beyond the buildings but it hovers as if it can’t decide.

For the first time she seems to see them there.

They look down at the white tabletop, up into the blue umbrella canvas, at the helicopter that can’t make up its mind. She disappears underwater. They can’t see all the way into the pool, into the water, but they can see enough and they wait for her to resurface. Playing with lighters, the sun almost done now, a dirty glow behind the buildings, waiting. One looks at his watch, another sits up straighter, taller, looking for her head. More waiting, drumming his fingertips on the table. And just as the one with the almost moustache pushes back his chair to get up, to step to the pool, to pull off his shoes and dive into the water to pull her unconscious body from the bottom, there is a whoosh of air as she breaks the surface. By now the other one has returned, aaaaahing down into his chair.

Finally, the call to prayer echoes and when it does they each reach into their pile of cellphone and lighter to retrieve a cigarette.

She is done swimming. She sits on her towel, glancing at them before giving her hair a good shake. They smoke and tap their lighters on the white tabletop, and the one says one last time, "*Haram*." But this time the others are too busy smoking to nod, taking in the smoke, holding it, and now blowing it up at the helicopter that hasn't stopped hovering.

The People of Nepal, or Maybe Tibet

I scurry to catch up with little Saud who once again has a cold, the snot worming down, gathering at his lip. And of course he thinks it great fun to run, zigzagging from coffee shop to coffee shop while Mum strolls behind and to the left, cellphone at her ear, urging me to "Catch him. His nose, his nose. Catch him."

Now he has found the moving sidewalk, and I jog alongside the railing—he on the rubbery moving side, me on the other. This, he thinks, is what going to the mall is all about: running and jumping and wearing his tiny sunglasses just like Mommy. Still jogging to keep up with him and his moving sidewalk, I carry two bags: one for his toys, treats, and extra clothes just in case; the other for her two pairs of shoes, Kleenex, water bottles, and extra makeup just in case. That, and strapped to my back, backpack style, is a neatly folded baby cart that I can easily unstrap, unfold for Saud when he grows weary and too tired to walk, run. To unsling it is simple, the wheels and plastic clicking into place. Meanwhile, Mum has slipped farther behind, cellphoning her sister in Surra about dinner on Friday and shopping on Saturday and then next week flying to London for somebody's birthday, or not.

Mondays, Wednesdays, and Fridays I wear something like purple pajamas, the other days, green—lime green. They prefer purple so they can find me at a glance—a quick scan, a splash of purple and there I am. The lime green is a little different; sometimes it takes more than a glance. When I wear the lime green I can't help but think of popsicles. Purple not so much—more like a bruise. Of the two, lime green is my favorite.

Little Saud catapults free of the moving sidewalk, loose once again, running between couples, scattering a small herd of teens, only slowing now and again to grin, to see if I am gaining. I have orders not to tug on his arm, not to the tell him to stop. Like a referee in a boxing match, I must hover around him and wait and see, and only interfere if danger is imminent. I don't know what the word imminent means but I can guess and be right. These are my orders from him, and sometimes her.

Yesterday I heard from Sally that Victoria couldn't do it anymore. The newspaper said that her sponsor had gone on vacation, locking her in the apartment. Passersby said she yelled down from the balcony for help, and they had yelled back, "What kind of help?" Shouting down that she had been locked in for three days—three days and three nights, and. . . . Passersby waving back up at her and walking on as if three days and three nights is nothing. The newspaper said that she jumped from a sixth floor apartment and that there would be an investigation. We shake our heads and cry because Victoria was a wonderful singer and her uncle knows my cousins in Leyte. But after the crying and the remembering, all we can do is get back to: "Have you heard from your family? How are your children? And your salary? When will you go home to visit?"

Saud slows, walks, stops to watch the fountain shoot jets of red water, to wipe his nose with the back of his hand, smearing a new line of snot across his cheek.

That night—after I cook their chicken and rice and peas just the way they like them, after I wash their dishes and find the newspaper that he can't find but that was "here a minute ago"; after I pick up their clothes and get Saud one last drink of water before bedtime—with everybody asleep so it is just me and the green-eyed cat—I watch a TV program about mountain climbing in Nepal or maybe Tibet. Although the commentator is not interested in discussing the mules that carry everything up the mountainside, there they are, roped together, carrying tents, water, food, pots and pans, everything that mountain climbers need. Petting that green-eyed cat, its purring under my hand, I watch the mules make their way up the rugged mountainside. The mules are led by the people of Nepal or maybe Tibet—either one, they are darker, smaller, and have whiter teeth than the mountain climbers who ride horses. The commentator says this is how these mountain people make money, make their living, by waiting for rich mountain climbers to come so they can lead their mules up the mountains. The commentator says they don't earn a lot of money, these people of Nepal or maybe Tibet—but enough. The program ends with the rich mountain climbers riding their horses, making their way over rocks, around boulders bigger than houses, to what will be base camp. They wave and smile at the camera. Behind them, in the distance, is a long line of mules with the smaller, darker people leading them by ropes. I have no desire to go to a place like that, to live that way. Petting the green-eyed cat to let her know how lucky I am.

The Doughnut Shop

A blue sleeve pegged with silver cufflinks slowly drifts in from the right. "Here, wanna read about Iraq?" Then, without waiting for a yes or no or . . . , the sleeve, with gold watch peeking out, drops the newspaper on the table.

"Certainly."

Smooth, almost eel-like, the sleeve pulls back. "It's the best paper around here, don't ya think?"

"Sure," and he fingers the front page to show the sleeve just how much he agrees.

Although the sleeve lingers—a shadowy blue line wavering at the corner of his eye—it has grown silent, and the only thing left for him to do is to look harder at the page, studying the words. Then, just when he might have to look up, the sleeve announces, "Right, well gotta go."

He continues to examine the front page, sip coffee and think of things that have nothing to do with newspapers. Some sort of green bug has landed on the tabletop, is walking across the tabletop, is headed straight for the newspaper. He lifts his fingers to let it go by. Finally, confident that the blue sleeve with gold watch and silver cufflinks has long since driven away, he folds the paper and drops it on the floor. "Certainly."

He had never cared for their doughnuts—pasty dough injected with bright-colored sugars—but their coffee is the best. The girls who make the doughnuts, who pour his coffee, who take out the garbage, don't care if he likes their doughnuts or not; they only know he is a quiet man who comes in three, sometimes four times a week. When their boss isn't looking—on his cellphone, staring out the window, into the harbor—they don't mind giving him a free cup of coffee every now and again. "Oh no, I'll pay," rustling the change in his pocket to prove it. "No, no, this one's on us," and she'll motion to the other girl, a soft freckled face. "Well, thank you." Smiles all around.

They are both small, delicate, and Filipina, and while the one is pretty in a cheerleader sort of way, the other isn't. They are strictly striped aprons, coffee, doughnuts and "Have a good day." That, and much giggling on Fridays. They are nothing like the doughnut shop in Salmiya.

In Salmiya, there was that time last winter, while sipping coffee and half-reading somebody's left-behind newspaper, that he overheard one of those loud Americans talking to the tall one. "Well, how about Saturday? Saturday night?" Huge hairy arms folded across a t-shirted chest, talking like he was angry but smiling like he wasn't. "Saturday? Well I don't know." Then unfolding his arms, shifting closer. "Saturday. Yes or no?" All the while she was looking down through the glass countertop, and then, with him edging closer, she reached in, pushing the cinnamon rolls closer together, putting the glazed doughnut in a straighter line. In the corner, right where the vents blow the coolest air, an old gray-*dishdasha* man sat hunched over his morning paper, reading it with a Sherlock Holmes magnifying glass. She started to pout and the American stroked his beard, and the old man turned the page, never once lifting his face from the magnifying glass.

Sipping his coffee, he thought about all the tall coffee shop waitresses he'd ever known. "I can't," she said, looking around to see who heard, who cared. "I just can't. I'd lose my job."

As he walked out, the American was leaning over the glass counter, his t-shirt riding up, showing the hairy square of his back.

It's been over a year since he left her. It really hadn't been such a difficult decision; he'd seen it coming from a long ways off, like watching a long-distance runner slowly, methodically, work his way toward the finish line. In the beginning, he thought it might have had something to do with money or the baby, but after a while he understood that it was none of those things. Even then it took another full year of planning, of waiting for the right time.

Katherine hadn't been a bad wife. She did all those things wonderfully well. But then there was that something else, that something that he didn't know the name for. *"Look at that," nudging him to look at the man waiting in line. "Look at that. How gross." Whispering now.*

He looked over and saw that the old man was picking his nose. He whispered back, "He's picking his nose."

"I know what he's doing, and I think it's gross, utterly gross." No whispering now. "There's a time and place for that kind of thing, and it's not here, not now."

And all he could do was turn and stare into the bank's wide-yawning vault.

"Mind if I sit here?"

"No, no, of course not," he answers.

She sits down and quickly, quietly, arranges her side of the table: newspaper to the right, glazed doughnut with milk to the left. A bite of doughnut, a sip of milk. She holds her newspaper to the side and slightly down in her lap. Another nibble of doughnut, followed by a careful folding of the front page.

Smiling into his coffee, he takes a gulp. Lukewarm. She has short pudgy fingers, and for a moment he is strangely disappointed. Another sip, the lukewarm having grown bigger; like taking a bitter medicine, he squints it down.

"That bad?"

He opens his eyes, and she is smiling at him.

"No, it's cold. I hate coffee that isn't hot." Smiling back at her, but knowing that her smile is better than his.

She nods, letting her lips pucker. A red scarf wraps her hair, there are large golden earrings. He smiles again, and this time it feels better, as if there's a silent contest going on and they are now tied. He has always liked women with pierced ears—something to do with the Mediterranean and Africa and the sun. Katherine refused to pierce her ears. Said it wasn't right for people to punch holes in their bodies. Said it was unnatural.

When he looks back, she is still puckering, her face staring up at the ceiling. A small ache rises to the rim of his throat. It is then that he surprises himself and says, "Would you care for some more coffee?"

Her face comes down, the pucker unrolling. "Oh no, none for me." And she motions to her milk.

"Of course."

There is a short space of watching one another before she begins to laugh. He hasn't been laughed at since Katherine. But this time it's different. In fact, seeing the clean white of her teeth, the bounce of golden earrings, he thinks that maybe there is something funny after all. He waits for her to finish.

Her scarf has slipped, undressing a brown wing of hair. Finally, he laughs with her, followed by another small piece of quiet.

"What's so funny?" he asks.

"I don't know. I mean, I'm not sure."

He nods and looks down into his empty cup.

"I mean for a moment there I felt like I was in a movie. One of those long gray French movies, where the man and the woman are sitting silently in the cafe, drinking, smoking, waiting for the rain to stop. You know the scene." Laughing some more. "I just thought I was somewhere else for a moment, that's all."

The headlines on her paper read: CAR BOMBS KILL SIXTY IN KARBALA.

"Right, just like an old movie."

"You know, I used to like coffee. Three, four cups a day."

He nods, waits, then remembers it's his turn. "What happened?"

"Nothing," her short fingers wiggling in the air to show him nothing. "I simply changed my mind one day."

He nods, even smiles, and then says, "What do you mean?"

Even before it's all out and done, he knows it's the wrong question. He watches to make certain, and yes, the friendliness slowly drains out of her eyes, her smile. She reaches up and tucks the long wisp back under the red scarf. A glance at the clock on the wall and she turns back to her paper.

"I suppose you think that's clever—the way you just sit there and nod? Condescending, is that it? Well it isn't clever, Martin. Not at all."

"Katherine, what do you want from me? Please tell me."

"Want? Oh Martin, why in God's name would I want anything from you?"

And then he would turn, looking out into the lawn, saying, "No, you're wrong, I'm a . . ."

But she wouldn't be hearing anymore, because the door would be wide open and she'd be gone. Towards the end, Katherine did a lot of walking out, driving off. He'd wait until he could no longer hear the car. Her getting up and driving away almost always made him heavy, tired.

He looks down at his empty cup and thinks back over the conversation. Perhaps he was trying too hard. Pushing back his chair, he steps to the counter, taking his place behind two young executives to get his refill.

" . . . and then the old man came walking out of his office, just like some old bear huffing out of its cave. He was out to get somebody, anybody, know what I mean?" Now digging into his pocket for change. "Ever since I've been there he's been that way—prowling about, sniffing for mistakes. Later, around ten or so, he begins to loosen up, but from eight-thirty to ten he's no good, know what I mean—no good." Both of them now smirking, nodding, looking down at their shoes. "Half dozen glazed and half dozen maple bars." Once the doughnuts are boxed, the two young executives politely argue over who will pay. With her apron looking almost too tight for her waist, the freckled-faced waitress takes the talker's money. As they head for the door, the talker laughingly says, "You owe me. Next time."

Holding out his empty coffee cup, he says, "Can I have a little more?"

"Sure, what do you say?"

"What?"

"What do you say?"

He blinks at the freckled-faced girl, and then says, "Please."

She laughs long and loud. "I'm just teasing." Reaching over to get the coffee pot, to fill up his waiting cup. "Just teasing." And now she blushes, as if she's not used to teasing.

He says, "Right. Thanks."

Putting the coffee pot back, still blushing and now giggling, saying one last time, "Just teasing."

A fat woman with her big-little son moves in behind him. She—*abayaed,* a glistening sweat under the chin—and he—less red, less sweaty but thicker—breathe heavily behind him.

"Thanks," and as he moves away, she, bumping his shoulder, steps up to take his place. His coffee storms.

"Give me a dozen cinnamon and some of these cream-filled, and . . ."

He sits down and thinks about fat people.

"Isn't that cute? Martin, isn't that cute?"

They were waiting at a red light and directly in front of them hobbled a tremendously fat husband and wife. He had a cane and she clung to him as if she needed one. Green light, with still half the street to cross. Horns honking.

"Isn't that darling."

When he looks up and sees that the son is watching him, a quiet panic comes over him. With one of those tiny wooden sticks, he stirs his coffee. The newspaper hides her face, but then she turns the page and a sliver of red peeks over the top. OIL HITS RECORD HIGH ABOVE $100. Once outside, the son says something to the mother, and she, a new sweat across her forehead, glares through the window at him.

He sips and goes on reading the back of her paper.

Their glaring complete, they get into their car. While the mother talks, her face growing wetter, redder, the son has opened the box of doughnuts, his face hidden behind the open box.

"Terrible," he says.

Slowly the newspaper comes down. "Were you speaking to me?"

"Oh no, I was just thinking out loud."

She checks her earrings, followed by a long drink of milk. He turns to look into the parking lot. Mother and son are gone.

"What I meant," she says, "was that one day I decided to stop drinking coffee, and that was that."

The way she places her hands flat against the tabletop makes her fingers look better, longer. He looks for a ring, and there are two, but neither is the married kind.

"That's all. I simply changed my mind. There's nothing wrong with that, you know."

He wonders how he ever could have thought her fingers stubby. "Of course. I didn't mean to pry."

Holding her head down and slightly to the right, she stares at the checkerboard linoleum. For the first time he looks hard at her face.

The cheerleader-pretty girl has walked out from behind the counter to clean the tables. She saves the newspapers, stacking them on the countertop. She works quickly, leaving their table for last.

"Still here?" Grinning down at him.

"Still here."

She laughs, her long hair wagging. Holding a damp dirty rag, she walks back to the counter and says something to the other girl. They giggle.

His second cup of coffee is almost gone, and she, her newspaper hanging off the table, continues to stare down at the floor. He likes this doughnut shop—always has—but he doesn't know why they think it's so funny he's still there.

The Lives of Poor People

He flashes his headlights to let me know it is him and although he is late he is here now and to step back because he is going to park right there, even closer, and when he does the brakes squeal like somebody's pig. He steps out of the van and asks if I'm the one who called and I say I am, and he shakes my hand but it means nothing, saying, "What happened?"

"Don't know. The red light flashed red and the next thing I knew the engine gave up and I rolled to the shoulder. It's a mystery."

He smiles at the mystery part.

Together, with flashlight, we look under the hood. He pulls at wires, rubber tubing, tsking every now and again. He says something about a gasket, but then changes his mind. "Transmission fluid." He redirects his flashlight to see under the car, the road, and the dark fluid that has puddled there. This earns his biggest, loudest tsk. He slams the hood shut, sighing, the flashlight beam hitting me full in the face. "You know this is the end of my shift," pointing at his wristwatch. I nod. A long line of cars rushes by, and we teeter in their wind. "The end of my shift and we don't get paid overtime—never have, never will."

I nod at this too but this time add, "I'm sorry."

More cars, one honking, two, no, three flashing their headlights. "It can't be fixed here, now, tomorrow maybe. Give me the keys and a truck will come out later." I do as I am told and drop the car keys into his outstretched hand. He then quickly does three things, one right after the other: turning his back to the traffic, switching off the light and answering his cellphone. "Hallow." His talk is loud, almost angry, and I understand only the No's and Yes's. Finally, "Come on, I'll take you home."

The van is a dirty white, and I have to wait until he clears off the seat, sliding bags and bottles and what looks like two tennis balls onto the floor. I look at the pile on the floor, and think something more needs to be said, after all it is the end of his shift and he is taking me home, and so, . . . "Your lunch?"

He glances at me and I motion to the bottles, bags. I mean it as some kind of joke, but he answers, "Yes, it's down there somewhere." I look to see if there's a smile or smirk, but he goes on. "The white bag on the right there . . . no, over one more, . . . there."

I reach down to pick it up and it's light, almost empty, yet something is there. Once I have hold of it I can only think of putting it back, the joke all used up, but he motions for me to take a look inside. "Go ahead."

Inside is a small bottle of once water, some celery, a plastic bowl of what could have been filled with almost anything. He sees me looking.

"Rice and carrots." Looking in the mirror and then at me. "That was my lunch. I have that and water, sometimes cola. My lunch."

"So no McDonald's for you, heh?"

It's not meant to be a funny but he laughs like it is—his white teeth caught in the middle of his bushy beard—and then says, "What somebody like you spends on a Big Mac with fries I can live on for three, maybe four days. One Big Mac with fries."

I look at him to see if he means it, but the lighting is all wrong and he hasn't stopped looking straight ahead, driving. He drives too slow for any Fourth Ring road, and it isn't long before the cars start stacking up behind us. "My shift is over, you know? A twelve-hour shift. Imagine. I'm tired, you know. Tired, but I'll take you home anyway. Don't get paid for overtime, none of us do."

I thank him but he only shrugs.

The rest of the way is filled with more flashing headlights and somebody sticking his head out the window to scream and gesture and then scream again. There is one last cellphone call before we arrive, and this time he does most of the listening until the end when he shouts one word and then flings the phone down on the seat between us.

When we get there he goes over the two speed bumps like they are not meant for him, bags and balls and cans and bottles hiccupping off the floor. Once he pulls over I hand him two dinar and he takes it like he is a clerk and I am buying groceries. He sees me looking down at his white lunch bag as I step out, and says, "It's OK, this is the way poor people live." I wait for more but there is nothing, he just lifts his hand goodbye.

Although it is late and I am tired and it's the end of his shift and he and his van lurch away and I know nothing about transmission fluid and almost everything about Big Macs with fries, I can't stop thinking about the paper bag with his used-to-be lunch.

13 February 2007

Organic shrapnel is bits and pieces of human flesh and bone flying outward with such velocity and ferociousness that they are wedged into the body of anyone within striking range.

He is watching a war movie, John Wayne in Vietnam, fighting the war. For two hours John Wayne and his men win a battle and then lose a battle and then, in the end, fight a battle that has no winner. After the third battle, he turns off the TV and goes into the bathroom to take another bath. Bathing is the best part of being away from Iraq. Once in the hot soapy water, he, like always, runs his fingers over his face, his jaw, along the swell of his throat, the meaty part of his left shoulder. In these places he feels the lumps, the tiny explosions of twisted flesh, and he will go on feeling them, say doctors. They take no special shape, these lumps, although early in the morning the big, shoulder one looks something like Florida, the others, longer, bigger. All of them have their own private ache in the evening. He is no longer afraid to touch them, to press into their spongy redness. The hot water helps.

Later he will go to the mall that he can see from his hotel window, and go to a coffee shop to sit and read the newspaper. Before he left they told him more than once not to wear any part of his uniform—no boots, no cap, nothing. "Civilian clothes only." Others are with him, some he knows, has joked with, others are nothing, just soldiers from North Carolina, Detroit, Seattle, Bakersfield, California. . . . Each one of them has his own hotel room for ten days. After that they must go back.

He walks straight to the first coffee shop he sees. For breakfast, he sips his coffee and picks at the four-dollar slice of chocolate cake. For the longest time he watches people cellphoning and smoking and more cellphoning. He hadn't expected this, this kind of being away from the war. They told him about something else, relaxation, swimming, girls who dressed and walked and talked like America. "Man, Marina Mall on a Friday night." And then he sees a little boy with mother, hand in hand, stopping to look into a shop window: polished black shoes, neatly arranged purses, belts with golden buckles. The boy, caring nothing for purses or belt buckles, watches his shoes, the shiny mall floor; something is there, red and bright, and of course he stretches to reach it, but she is a mother and hangs on tight—his fingertips straining, almost there but not quite. No longer interested in his slice of cake, sipping lukewarm coffee, and yet it seems important that he keep watching. He holds the cup to his lips but does not drink. He spies one of the others, Seattle, walking the other side of the mall, and quickly he buries his face into somebody's forgotten newspaper, staring into stock market numbers.

Once Seattle is gone, his fingers, like always, return to his jaw, the red swells just behind the soft of his earlobe. Coffee cup in one hand, his jaw in the other. The little boy with mother is still there, she looking through the glass, now tapping it with her fingernails, he continuing to almost touch . . . and it was then that Sergeant Brown had yelled, "NO! NO!" . . . , that the family with daughters and sons had stepped into the middle of the street to give their patrol plenty of room, . . . that the smallest son with a red Mickey Mouse sweater was tapping the road with a stick, not even a stick but a small branch, and now done tapping long enough to smile, gawking up at him, at all of them, and that out of nowhere and right behind the family steps a man from the alleyway, a man whose *dishdasha* is all wrong: too dirty, too tight, a man who is looking up at the sky, hands on chest, but looking straight up into the sky, talking to the sky . . . ; and Sergeant Brown hasn't stopped yelling "NO, NO, NO," only louder, bigger, . . . but of course it is too late. The air is frantic with sound, a spasm of redyellowwhite, a gush of furnace heat. His sunglasses snap at the nose, jumping into the air, the hot grabbing him like a red fever, eating into his face and shoulders. His helmet is ripped from his head. A red hot spray pitches him ridiculously sideways. A new heat claws at his face and arms. His gloves are on fire. In the end, there is only dust and a car horn that won't stop.

Somewhere, someone knocks over a glass, or maybe an ashtray, and its tiny explosion has him gripping the table, his heart racing, his coffee storming. Like a kind of braille, running his fingers over the fleshy knobs along his neck, the tiny eruptions up and down his cheek, the soft part behind his earlobe. By now the little boy has given up trying to reach the shiny bright as he and his mother move to the next shop, the next window: scarves the color of peacocks. Feeling the ache along his jaw, the red swell of flesh, and seeing a boy with a stick. He runs his hand over his head. They say the hair will never grow back on the left side, that his left ear will never work again. He must learn to live with headaches.

It has been three days now, and already he knows he will not stay ten days, knows he cannot sit at coffee shops for ten days sipping coffee, nibbling wedges of cake. Although he will miss the baths, two maybe three times a day, he must go back early, back to Baquba and Kirkuk, the long list of villages whose names he'd forgotten, never known. Now, carefully, secretly, he slips a hand under his open shirt, his fingers once again feeling the swelling that has grown then shrunk and now grown again. Hand at his throat, the lumps in his cheeks, forever part of a little boy with red Mickey Mouse sweater.

Backyard Readings

It was one of those books that refused to get better: tales of a dysfunctional family whose father only brushes his teeth on Fridays, after prayers, whose mother thinks she's half Chinese when she isn't, whose sons and daughters stay out all night, never cut their hair, think school is some kind of political conspiracy, and so on. I wanted it to get better, even gave it a second chance, a whole line of second chances, but by the time I was tired of giving it second chances I was almost done with it, another two or three chapters. On my way to the back porch, I pick it up from the counter and step warmly into a Wednesday afternoon.

After two or three pages of reading but not reading, my feet propped on the other chair, the sun working sleepily on my face, the sliding glass door whispers open, and out she steps wearing her mother's favorite black boots. I put the book in my lap and watch her clunk across the patio. I think about warning her not to scuff them, but the sun and the reading but not reading has made me especially tired and uncaring, so I just watch. That's when she takes three giant steps my way, and, staying in the shade, sits down, stretching out on the cool cement. Now I have no choice but to say something about the boots, and I do and she says, "*Sah*." It's right after her *sah* that Blackie walks out from under the rose bushes where he's been hiding, watching, waiting, and goes straight to her to let her know he wants to be rubbed. This is almost better than wearing Mom's boots, she says, because Blackie never goes to her unless it has something to do with food. After a good many strokes along Blackie's back, playfully pulling his tail, she says Blackie should be an indoor cat, and that if he was she'd take care of him, feed him, change the litter box—everything. After she is done making him a happy indoor cat, I say no. "Blackie is an outdoor cat, always has been, and besides, he wouldn't care for being surrounded by all that soft carpet, squeezing in behind bookcases and chairs. . . . He'd miss his outside, the weeds and grass and dirt." She nods, but even I can tell it has nothing to do with agreement, and so she gets up, the black boots making it extra difficult, and reopening the sliding glass door extra wide, stands back, giving Blackie plenty of room. At first Blackie ignores the invitation, but seeing some chair leg to rub against, it isn't long before he slowly looks at it again, like it's a trap but then relooking, closer, thinking that if it is a trap it can't be much of one. To help Blackie make up his mind she clunks her way back into the house and sits down on the soft carpet. Blackie can't help himself and steps toward the door and then backs up, sniffing, tip-toeing, going half way in, half way out, and just when it looks as if he won't be fooled, goes all the way in. I hear her say something to Blackie but then she makes the mistake of getting up with those big black boots and when she does Blackie bolts out the door, across the porch, disappearing under the rose bushes.

When she comes back out I can see where she has scuffed the boots. Nothing serious, nothing that can't be polished, wiped clean. This time I ask her how school is.

"OK."

"Anything important happening?"

"*Lah.*"

"How about tomorrow? What's going on at school tomorrow?"

"Nothing."

"How about the day after tomorrow, and the day after that?"

"Nothing."

These are old questions, older answers.

She can see Blackie watching her from under the bushes. From here, if you look just to the left of the palms, you can see the tips of two minarets, and beyond that, through the milky heat, the highrises of downtown. A tiny wind has found its way through the palms, over the fence, teasing her hair. I watch her hair swirl, and she smiles.

The call to prayer fills the air.

And so it goes as she continues to clunk around in her mother's boots, walking first this way then that and then onto the lawn where the clunking changes into *thunking.*

In no hurry to return to my book, I say, "Won't be long now."

"What?"

"Middle School next year. New school. That's a big step, you know. More responsibility. More everything."

The call to prayer filling the air.

"Time for you to start making some decisions."

The wind fingering the roses.

"Know what I mean? Time to make some important decisions."

She has turned to watch herself in the glass door, turning sideways like one of those models, chin on shoulder, tossing her head to make her hair swish. By now the sun is at the top of the fence so even squinting doesn't help. That's when I forget about the book in my lap, and although I make a grab, it topples, fluttering birdlike. And she says, "Blackie would make a good indoor cat. He's just scared that's all. A little scared."

I nod, squinting, looking in her direction, the tiny wind relentless, toying with her hair.

With Blackie somewhere under the rose bushes and the sun dazzling atop the fence, she slips off the boots and stares good and hard at the gray scuff on the toe. She rubs it once, twice, and it is gone. "There."

"There."

She turns to look for Blackie, and not seeing him, goes back to rubbing her mother's boots. That's when she starts to cry.

When I squat next to her on the cool cement, I take her hand and say, "What's wrong? Where does it hurt?"

Rubbing her mother's favorite black boots, pushing the hair out of her eyes even though it isn't in her eyes, she says, "I don't know."

And the call to prayer fills the air.

The Late Breakfast

The sign reads: Breakfast daily 7-12.

So when he comes walking in at 2 in the afternoon and says he'd like breakfast, and the waitress points at the sign, saying, breakfast was over two hours ago, "I'm so sorry," he doesn't like it.

That's when he slowly unstrings the surgical mask from his face, undoing one ear at a time because a sandstorm has been churning all day, and now brushing off his shoulders with one hand and then the other. Already now, he says it again, "I want breakfast."

"Sorry. Breakfast is over, sir."

"I want breakfast."

"Sorry."

With the second sorry, he looks at her and then at the sign and then back at her. All the while, she smiles, as trained. Finally, he slowly removes his sunglasses, folding them neatly, quietly on the tabletop, saying, "You have something like a manager here?"

"Yes."

"This is good. Bring him to me." Pointing his finger straight down at the tabletop.

"Actually sir it's a she not a he."

His finger still pointing straight down, "Bring her to me."

There are others, in the back, away from the windows. Two what-look-to-be high school girls are hunched over a piece of paper, giggling. Next to them, near a huddle of potted plants, sits a family—milkshakes for everybody.

And the waitress, having done her duty, hurries to the back room and almost immediately returns with someone just like her, only bigger, but with pencils in her pocket and wearing a red bowtie.

"Yes sir, how may I . . ."

"You realize do you not whose country you are living in? *Sah?*"

"Yes sir, but how may I . . ."

"Allow me to answer for you," rubbing his forehead as if to push back a headache. "It is very simple, maybe almost too simple. It goes like this: this is my country," hands to his chest to show her. "You are just visiting here, working but visiting, *Sah?* So, for all general purposes, I pay your salary. I pay all your salaries," waving his hand towards the grill and beyond. "My country. I grew up here, right over there," motioning toward the waters of the gulf. "My family is here, my father and grandfather helped build and develop this country—from nothing to something. Before oil, before the Invasion, before you were born. And you? You are here for, what, three maybe four years, and in the meantime you take our money and what, send it back home. Western Union every month? To assorted mothers and fathers and cousins, and maybe a child or two? Am I right?"

As he speaks he looks at his sunglasses, sometimes lifting his eyes to glare at her bowtie. His hands are now clasped on the tabletop, next to the napkins and the salt and pepper shakers. On the wall above his head is another sign, saying, No Smoking Please.

"The Philippines, Mumbai, Jakarta, Pakistan. It doesn't matter. It's all the same. So," . . . and now reaching down into his *dishdasha* to unload cigarettes, lighter, cellphone, *misbaha,* wallet, arranging all precisely around his sunglasses. "So, one more time, you work for me. *Sah?* You work for me and you are visitors and thank you for coming but when you go back home I will still be here, and so I want my breakfast and I want it now. That sign out there on the window does not apply to me. Others?" Lighting a cigarette and taking a deep gulp of smoke, until, all done gulping, he lets it trickle from his nostrils, "Others, Americans, Brits, sure, of course, but me—us?"

The manager, her nametag reads Sally, waits, all the while smiling, nodding. Sally is not a manager for nothing. She knows what is what, and so turning to the waitress who has not stopped hovering at her shoulder, she smilingly says, "Please bring the gentleman the breakfast menu."

But before the waitress can turn to go, he says, "No need for that, no need," bringing his cigarette hand up like he is stopping traffic. "No need, I want two eggs sunnyside up, coffee, and fried potatoes—an extra portion of fried potatoes." His order delivered he now turns to his cellphone because it is ringing. She writes everything on a pad of white paper.

They bring him his breakfast of eggs sunnyside up with coffee and extra fried potatoes, and in the end, as he lights another cigarette, as he gets up to leave, they have to stop him at the door, reminding him that he hasn't paid yet.

The Excellent Teacher

When he wakes in the early morning, it is already hot. The call to prayer has come and gone, and it is hot and the air conditioning, although running all night, every night, no longer makes a difference but simply pushes warm air from room to room. His breakfast is coffee shops and Filipino waitresses who have been trained to say Good morning and Thank you and Come again. Sometimes he asks them how they are, and almost always they stop to stare, smiling, looking secretly surprised that anyone would care. Once he finishes his coffee and toast and reads bits and pieces of the newspaper and pays and heads for the door, they say, "Come again." And he says he will. After the coffee shop the traffic is thicker, heavier, like a kind of syrup. He has learned that the honking and gesturing and face-making, the flashing headlights, have almost nothing to do with the traffic. It has to do with something else, something he doesn't have a name for yet.

He is a teacher. Always has been, never thought of anything else, except when he was ten years old and was convinced that being a cowboy or explorer, or even a baseball player, might be a better idea. Ten years old. Once upon a time he thought he was a good teacher, at times even excellent, but now, with this teaching in the Arab World, he isn't so sure.

As he sits in his car, waiting, he thinks back to yesterday's student. It is not an important remembrance but something to think about while the traffic makes up its mind.

When he looked up, a head with *hijab* was leaning into his doorway, whispering, "Hello." Quickly, the rest of her body follows, properly filling the doorway, followed by another "Hello?" He motions for her to "Come in." That is when she does three things in one seamless motion: she sits down, says "Thank you," and begins to cry. Although she is covered, wisps of brown hair peek out. Tears roll down her cheeks, finding the corners of her mouth.

Of course he knows her, has watched her take the same seat in the back of the classroom, near the window, every Sunday, Tuesday, Thursday, has watched her painfully remove her cellphone from the desktop and slip it into her bag. When he chances a glance in her direction, she nods. He has read her assignment, spreading her paper out in front of him on the kitchen table, reading until by mid-page he realized it was one endless sentence, without punctuation, without prepositions, with three, no, four verbs. . . . Reading on, waiting, wanting it to make sense, hoping it will come together in some magical way at the end. At the bottom of the page, out of space, it stopped. Pushing himself away from the kitchen table, he turned to look out the window. There was a sandstorm, the air filled with the color of butterscotch. Returning to her paper, he wrote, "This is a very long non-sentence."

Before she can properly begin, she wonders if he might have some tissues. "Do you have tissues?"

"Certainly. Here."

Now ready, she tells him the story of how her family has been going through a terrible divorce, how her father no longer lives at home, but somewhere in Jordan, with another, younger wife, "young enough to be my older sister," and not only that, but the maid of five years has disappeared, taking all of Mom's favorite jewelry with her. Clenching tissues in her fist. And just last week, her grandmother, "Who's always been my best friend and the light of my life," has been diagnosed with breast cancer, and, "*Ya'ni,* the morning traffic is so bad that it's almost impossible to get to class on time" and so, "You, *ya'ni,* can see that this final grade is not my fault, even unfair, don't you think?"

As she tells her story, her eyes move back and forth between him and the window. Finally, thinking he must be missing something, he turns to see what she sees: boats and blue water, the all-familiar haze, buildings that are forever in mid-construction. Turning back to her, she continues, hasn't stopped, and he listens, nodding at the right times. When she finishes, wondering if he has any more tissues, he asks, "And you have a large family?"

He knows this has nothing to do with anything, but remembering her paper, her long non-sentence, he asks it anyway.

"Two sisters and one brother."

He sighs, as if yes, he has made up his mind, and facing her asks, "Yes, and how is Mohammad?"

She stops in mid-tearing to look at him, moving her red lips once, twice, until finally, "How do you know my brother? He is only ten? How do you know him?" This, somewhere between a question and a demand.

As they both wait, another student suddenly appears at the door, knocking and then stepping into the office, as if to say "the knocking part doesn't really mean anything, just a fake knock because I'm inviting myself in anyway." This student wants him to sign a form, holding the paper out to him. "Here." He takes it, reads it, signs it and the student walks away happy.

Alone again with her, he says, "This has been a very nasty semester for you." She agrees, although he is certain she does not know the word nasty.

After what seems a very long time, like one of her non-sentences, he says there is nothing he can do and wishes her good luck, and although he has no meeting to go to he tells her he does. "In fact, I'm late for a meeting." She quickly stands, and hands him the tissues she didn't use. He stands to show her how serious he is about going to the meeting. At the door she hesitates, half-turning to say one last thing but then, at the last moment, seems to change her mind, and walks away. He knows why she hesitated, what she wanted to ask but didn't.

Frankly, he expected her sooner. There were other students yesterday. Some like Fatma, most not. He tries to remember what he has taught them, what they might have learned, what they can use. But he does not remember teaching them anything. He does not remember saying anything that would make a difference. He talks, they nod. He does not remember any of their final grades. But he does know their names, and that must count for something. He thinks something is terribly wrong that he does not remember what he has taught them, what they have learned. Out of all those weeks, three classes every week, he only remembers writing: "This is a very long non-sentence."

The Emergency Room Doctor at Play

He doesn't know it—how could he—but see that boy over there, the one who's too big for the swing, whose feet drag every time he goes across the monkey bars, who's not used to waiting his turn for anything? In another twenty-two years, he's the one who'll be saying—yet again—Mubarak's dead.

That's right, it'll start off with him throwing open the emergency room doors, bellowing, "Now what?" No time for scrubbing, no time for masks or caps, and the best he can do is snap on gloves as he hears, "No pulse. Nothing." The nurse says it not once but twice. So everything is ready for what must be next, and with Mubarak flat on his back, his *dishdasha* neatly scissored down the middle, his white chest caught in the clean gleam of surgical light, the doctor will say, "Clear." But none of the nurses will have to move because they'll already be clear, away from the table, arms folded, watching, and the thud of electricity will send Mubarak wiggling jello-like. But nothing will come of it. And so, again, "Clear," and Mubarak will buck again. Still nothing. Finally, after stopping long enough to press two fingers against Mubarak's neck, waiting, and then demanding a number three scalpel from a nurse who has never liked him, he'll make a nice straight slice down the middle of Mubarak's hairless chest and reaching in and under—the blood jumping everywhere—grab hold of Mubarak's heart, squeezing, in a futile attempt to get it going, just one good throb will do. The nurses, amid catheters and syringes and tubing, have not moved from their stations, watching him do the stuff of movies. Minutes later, on a Thursday, with the unfriendly nurse moving over to stand in the doorway, he'll turn and slowly lifting his bloody hand out of Mubarak's chest announce, "He's dead." The nurse, out of habit, will look up at the big clock on the wall and say, "1:10."

Yep, he's the one all right. Long sandy hair in his eyes, and what looks like the beginning of buck teeth; and how about the way he's squinting when there's not a glint of sunshine anywhere. There are glasses to be had. In another 21 years and ten days, he'll be the one—after all those years of medical school in Ireland and student loans and almost falling in love and coming close to a nervous breakdown not once but twice—he'll be working the night shift at the Al Hadi Hospital, hoping for one quiet night, just this once, because after two nights of apartment fires and head-on collisions he's exhausted. But it's not to be. In the first place, Amer, the new intern, will be out with the flu while Maggie, at the last minute, will call in with an emergency of her own: unfriendly newly-divorced husband with kids. And so a little after midnight, they'll wheel in poor overweight Mubarak, medics yelling out a blood pressure that isn't there, hasn't been since Salmiya. But wheeling him in, saying, "He's too young for heart failure. It has to be something else. Has to be." The green flicker of the ambulance filling the hallway.

So there he is: blue shirt with bluer jeans, red stars on his tennis shoes. He doesn't look like a doctor, does he? Course you can't tell at his age, but hear all that yelling, "A dare's a dare. You've got to do as I say. *Sah. Sah?*" See that boy on the slide, the one wearing the Manchester United t-shirt? Better watch out because his nose is about to be bloodied. Nothing doctorly here.

All the while, Mubarak, sitting over there in the shade, is half watching his four-year-old daughter in the sandbox—not really a sandbox, more like a pile of sand—and half reading a magazine article about the life and times of Failaka Island, of ancient ruins, bullet-riddled walls, the same page over and over, thinking of things that have nothing to do with Failaka Island or daughters playing in the sand. Mubarak is smoking, one cigarette after the other—not even waiting for the one to grow ashes before thinking of smoking another. Nothing new here, because he has smoked since he was twelve, even eleven if you count that one time behind the chalet, first secretly, then openly, with friends. In the beginning, his mother was angry with him, but after the third time she gave up. His father shrugged, smirked, "Boys."

Finally, as he puts the magazine down, reluctantly crushing his unfinished cigarette in the sand, he walks over to break up the fight that's made good the bloody nose; and it isn't long before the emergency room doctor-to-be, having never stopped insisting that "A dare's a dare. *Sah, Sah?*", is now trying his best to pull free of a Mubarak who's got a good grip on his shirt. Mubarak has heard enough, his four-year-old daughter has heard enough, and so he says, "Enough. . . . Watch your language, . . ." Suddenly, there's a ripping, and Mubarak steps back with a handful of empty blue sleeve. Everything stops. The boy stares at his sleeveless shirt, and then, finding a new anger, says, "Look what you did. Why'd you do that? *Laish?*"

Mubarak turns to give the sleeve back, mumbling, "Sorry, didn't mean to, but . . ."

The someday-emergency room doctor snatching his sleeve out of Mubarak's hand and, no longer caring about the bloody-nosed double-darer, yells at Mubarak, "My mom will go crazy. She'll kill you."

Mubarak, not wanting to think he really means it—after all he's only nine, maybe ten—walks back to the bench, to another cigarette, to his magazine and daughter who has never stopped playing in the sand.

The boy walks away too. But as he leaves, he jerks a thumb in Mubarak's direction and says to nobody special, "My mother will go wild. He's dead. *Mayit*."

Somewhere on the Gulf Road

I sweep sand. Actually that isn't entirely true, a piece of the truth. I sweep sand and pebbles and dirt off the streets and when there isn't any sand I pick up gum wrappers and cigarette butts and tissues and plastic bottles and crusts of bread—anything that doesn't belong. I wheel about one of those battered bluegray garbage containers from here to there; if it's especially hot I'll sometimes park my container in the shade and wait for the garbage to appear.

Every morning at the shed I give Mr. Khan an extra one dinar so he'll feel better about thumbing through that chart of his before finally pulling out his pencil and assigning me an intersection. Not even a real intersection, anything with a stoplight will do. As a rule I'm a fast learner, and so it only took me two or three days to understand the importance of stoplights and white faces. In fact, you could say I've learned to specialize in white faces, the way I linger around their cars while they're waiting for the light to change, the way I'll stop to pick up some invisible bit of paper, twigs—anything will do. That, and it's important to glance at them in a certain way; staring is no good, and almost never works. But hover about their cars, even smile, as if this sweeping the sands of Kuwait is nothing. And sometimes they'll motion for me to come closer, sometimes nothing more than rolling down the window. Every now and again they'll give coins to their children to hand to me. Like feeding the animals at the zoo, they giggle and squeal.

Sweeping the dirt and dust of Kuwait isn't so bad. There's money to be found. Coins in the dust. How about the time I found a neatly folded ten dinar bill under a heap of broken glass, or that Tuesday morning in April when I discovered five dinar wrapped neatly around a twig. Sometimes there are things that have nothing to do with money: that windy afternoon I reached down and picked up somebody's brown, dusty thumb, the way I had to hold it up to the sunlight because I couldn't believe somebody's thumb would just be curled up in the gutter like that. Of course there's the heat, and the boys with their Lamborghinis and Ferraris saying things they really don't mean but they have to say because, after all, they're boys with their friends. Being young, it's part of their job; I was the same . . . but different. And so I smile and nod, and wheel my garbage cart away from their cars, just in case. Besides, for every "Paki go home," there's the businessman who will motion me over, zip down his window and press 250 *fils* into my hand. They rarely say anything, these people who give money. Maybe a "Here." "Good luck." or "Good job." But really, what's to say?

Every morning before sunrise, the ragged once-school bus picks us up at the water tower and takes us to the shed where we collect our tools and containers, where we slip into our bright yellow jumpsuits. I've seen the same kinds of jumpsuits on prisoners, convicts. The shed: it has everything we'll need for the day. I could ask for a container with bigger newer wheels, or a broom with stronger bristles that sweep, but Mr. Khan cares nothing for things like that unless there's one or two dinar in the morning handshake. We won't see Mr. Khan until the evening, when we return to the shed with our tools and yellow jumpsuits.

Jabran, my cousin, works at the mall, in the parking lot. We've got the same job except his garbage container is black and they give him a broom and sometimes a tiny shovel. As he brushes and shovels, he'll stop every now and again to point out parking places to drivers. He holds his broom like a pointer. Sometimes they'll give him money because he points out parking places that unless they're blind they'd see anyway. He never gets angry if they give him nothing, ignore his existence. He understands. In a different time and place he'd probably do the same thing. We all would. Like me, Jabran's a fast learner, too. After they park, he knows better than to stand right next to their car, the timing, positioning is important, close but not too close, behind and to the right, reaching down to pick up a paper that isn't there. He tells the story of that morning when, like always, he was pointing out parking spaces with his broom handle and some American walked up to him and slapped two dinar into his hand, telling him, "Get something to eat." Two dinar for pointing out a parking space. It made him change his mind about Americans.

At the end of the day, as the dirty yellow once-school bus takes us back to where we belong, to the shed where we return our tools, dump our garbage, take off our bright yellow jumpsuits, we sometimes joke about how we have jobs for the rest of our lives. The way people think nothing of tossing cigarettes and papers and bottles out of their cars so we can have jobs. It's nice of them to think of us. And of course there's always the sand.

The Soor Street Insurance Company

Her name is Nooriyah but almost everybody called her Noor or Yah, or maybe Ri. Nobody knew why she'd settle for almost anything but Nooriyah. After all, Nooriyah is a good strong Islamic name. A lot of good women are named Nooriyah, or at least should be.

Ri's been with us for years—ten, eleven years, who's to count. She's an accountant. Her desk is in the back, against the wall, next to the gray metal fuse box. Almost everybody says she should get away from that fuse box and move closer to the rest of us. When you least expect it there could be sparks, a fire, electricity flying every which way. You never know. But Ri only smiles, saying things like, "Don't worry," or "Everything will be all right." Can you imagine?

With a name like Ri you'd think she'd have long black hair. If not jet black then the darkest of browns for sure. But no, not our Ri, her hair's something like a red, with wisps of gray here and there. That, and Ri doesn't smoke but looks like she should; there's that something around the mouth that hints of cigarette-tough. She looks like she should belong to somebody's bowling team, or maybe a softball league. But that's our Ri for you: looking one way while acting another.

It was that first Tuesday in April when Ri finally decided to do something that finally came close to matching the way she looked:

she came to work wearing slippers. They kidded her. Ri's wearing slippers. Ri's wearing slippers. Isn't that a hoot. Good old Ri. Ha. Even Yousef, the office manager, thought it was a good one. Good old Ri. Springtime in the office. But then she did it again, two days in a row, then three, and into the next week. Five days in a row of Ri wearing her pinkandwhite slippers to the office. After day three, Yousef no longer thought it funny. He's a young manager, Yousef is, twenty-six, but he knows when to laugh, and when not to, and when day three of Ri and her slippers came around Yousef waited until the ten o'clock break, and then—the coast being clear—approached her, saying, "That was a good joke, but let's not go overboard on this, Ri, know what I mean. Enough is enough." Because he's only twenty-six, and not at all sure office managering is for him, he said all this with a smile, looking down and shuffling his feet and, smiling one last time, saying manager-like, "Ri, enough is enough, know what I mean?"

Ri nodded, saying she knew exactly what he meant, but then went on to say, "It's my feet. My feet have changed, almost overnight they've changed. They're not liking my shoes. They swell up, get rashy, it must have something to do with the leather, the heat, who knows. Even the foot doctor doesn't know. See, . . ." And she handed him a note from the foot doctor, a note that in so many big medical words said her feet no longer cared for shoes, that she would have to wear slippers, for the time being. Thank you very much. Dr. Krishnan.

Yousef read the note once, twice, and said he'd be right back but, Oh, by the way, would she mind if he made a copy of this, "You know, just in case?"

"Be my guest."

About this time small herds of pigeons started to lounge around the windows. Every now and again they'd whirlwind away, spooking Eman, whose desk is up against the glass, coffee jumping out of her cup, staining her desk. There were two days of warm rain. But there's more. Dalia finally had her seven pound baby girl but was having a terrible time breastfeeding. Meanwhile, Amer Hassaan had missed two days straight because of his mother's cancer; and then three more days that had nothing to do with mothers or cancer. On day six he strutted into the office like nothing had happened. It wasn't long after that that Amer was called into Mr. Jordan's office for a long talk. When he came out he was more red-eyed than when he went in.

April continued, and so did Ri's pinkandwhite slippers. By then, nobody said anything or thought much about it. They had their own problems: unpaid bills, unfriendly neighbors, killings in Africa, bedwetting daughters, and so on. Who's to care about someone like Ri who thinks slippers are better than shoes?

But then one day in May, not long after almost everybody stopped caring about Ri and her slippers, Ms. Akbar went to Yousef. Yousef had just had a birthday, twenty-seven now, the office secretively passing around a happy birthday card to sign: "Good luck." "You're the best." "Happy birthday." But Ms. Akbar wasn't there about his birthday; she was there because she didn't like it. Not one bit.

Yousef, busy looking at flow charts, looked up at Ms. Akbar, and said, "Don't like what?"

She answered, "Ri."

Yousef, still half-thinking about flow charts, said, "Ri?"

"Yes, Ri."

Yousef put down the charts to make sure he was getting it right before saying again, "You don't like Ri?"

"No, no," said Ms. Akbar. "Not Ri. Her slippers. It's not right."

Pushing the charts all the way to the right so he could give her room, he said, "What do you mean?"

Ms. Akbar went on, "She and those slippers of hers shuffling over the linoleum floor. It's irritating and bothersome and not right, and I don't like it."

Yousef nodded, saying, "I see."

"Besides"—saving her best point for last—"besides, it's not very professional, now is it? Is it?"

Yousef hadn't stopped nodding, "I see."

But Ms. Akbar was not used to 'I sees' making a difference. After all, she'd grown up in a three-bedroom Beirut apartment with five brothers and three sisters, and knew all about the right and wrong of things like space and noise and irritation, and so, folding her arms across her chest—smothering that silver necklace of hers—she waited.

Yousef nodded, but this time more to himself than to her, and when he saw that his nodding and I-seeing weren't going to make a difference, he shuffled papers and said, "I'll look into it."

This, thought Ms. Akbar, was better than an "I see," and with that she said, "All right," and walked out of his office and back to a desk cluttered with photographs of children and grandchildren and one dead husband.

Ms. Akbar complained three, four more times to Yousef about Ri's slippers, and each time Yousef—now thinking he knew how to handle Ms. Akbar—said, "Yes, I see, I'll look into it."

Finally, Ms. Akbar grew tired of his not looking into it, and said, "I'll quit . . . I'll quit if something isn't done about her slippers. I'll quit."

At this point Yousef didn't say he'd look into it, instead he said, "Ms. Akbar, there's nothing to be done." What he didn't say was that he was afraid of lawsuits, discrimination charges, and finally, that he'd lose his job. Twenty-seven, with twin boys, and jobless. Not a pretty picture. All of this he didn't say, only, "There's nothing to be done."

Ms. Akbar, warming to the situation, said, "Fine, then I quit."

But Yousef, not wanting to lose Ms. Akbar—because although she didn't like the shuffling of slippers, she was still a damn fine secretary—said, "Wait." All the while her hand had a good grip on the doorknob, showing him how it'd better be good because she'd walk out and into another job if it wasn't; and he, almost as if it was an idea he'd been working on for a long time, and only now, now that it had come down to this, does he dare to say it, half-rising from his chair, said, "I've got an idea."

Later that week, two carpet men came in and put down a beige carpet, covering all the good cool linoleum. It took them all day and part of the next, but by noon on Wednesday the entire office had a new thick beige carpet. On Thursday Ri came in with her pinkandwhite slippers and found that they didn't work on carpet. She couldn't shuffle. Ms. Akbar waited and watched and was pleased in a Beirut way.

But Ri, still not knowing her slippers bothered anybody, how could they, slippered as best she could into Yousef's office, and said, "Good carpet."

Yousef waited, knowing there had to be more.

But Ri just said good carpet and then, "However, beige shows the dirt. Did you know that?"

Yousef nodded.

It was then, as Ri turned to go, that she said one last thing that I'm sure has puzzled Yousef ever since—wherever he is. Looking straight at Yousef, like he was suddenly something other than just some young office manager, she said, "By the way, Yousef, I'd like to be called by my real name from now on if you don't mind. Nooriyah. From now on call me Nooriyah."

Later, once we began to call her Nooriyah, they said that Ms. Akbar had never liked Ri, or Nooriyah, not since day one. According to Ms. Akbar's Beirut thinking, it had something to do with her being in the back, by the fuse box, like she was too good for the rest of us.

It wasn't long after the new carpet and Ri wanting her old name back that Yousef quit. Said he had another, better job offer. Some of us weren't so sure "quit" was the right word. After all, Mr. Jordan, the vice-president, had always thought Ms. Akbar something extra special. The last two office parties had shown us that.

We had a small going-away party for Yousef Thursday before last. Everybody stayed after work to toast his new job. It was right after the third or fourth toast that Ms. Akbar spilled Coca Cola all over the new carpet. Yousef told her not to worry, but Ms. Akbar insisted on being terribly sorry anyway.

The Censor

Wanted: *Seeking someone who is not too young, not too old. Successful candidate must know the ways of the world. Looking for somebody who possesses good moral sense, someone who knows decency when sees it. The successful candidate must know how to use a black magic marker.*

Once Fatemah got the job, her supervisor, Mr. Nassir, pushed back his chair, stood up, and said, "Congratulations, you've got the job." He went on to say how she would have to get up early in the morning, and be ready to go to work tomorrow, because, "work like this cannot wait. Don't you agree?" And she did. "Oh, by the way," he continued, "don't worry about bringing any markers, we have plenty, but, again, come early, around 4 am, because that's when the foreign newspapers and magazines are flown in; and another thing, there will be days when there won't be much to do, to mark, and when that happens we might ask you to do something else, something more, but never mind, let's wait and see because usually there's always something: a wine bottle here, too much cleavage there." Fatemah nodded. But Mr. Nassir wasn't done. "This is a daily issue, this censoring business—every day. So, be at the airport at 4 am, terminal one, room D33. The newspapers are delivered in big silver trucks fresh off flights from London and Paris, even Washington DC. No doodling, no smiley faces. This is serious stuff." Finally, all done, he held out his hand to have her shake it, and she did, although she'd never shaken many men's hands.

Fatemah ended with, "Thank you for this opportunity."

He replied, "Not at all, it's nothing."

The next morning—her two children and husband plus maid still asleep—Fatemah with driver makes her way to the airport. Only after much asking and wrong directions and re-asking does she finally find room D33 where stacks of foreign newspapers await her. Picking up the first newspaper, it doesn't take her long to find what she is looking for. On page 13, something called the Culture section, there is an announcement for a photo exhibition in Berlin, some ministry of arts and sciences, and to prove it there is somebody's wonderfully large photo of Michelangelo's *David*. On the table, to her left, is a row of ten black markers and she grabs the closest, blackest one, uncaps it, and begins work. Quickly, smoothly, expertly, as if she has been doing this for years, she gives David the long black shorts he deserves. "Yes, that's better." Moving on now, page 15, and there is a fashion show: Milan, Spring Collection; six photos of long skinny-legged models, staring straight into the camera, as if even the hint of a smile is all wrong. Glaring into the lens, these girls. But never mind, it is their too short dresses and see-through blouses that need fixing. And so, without a second thought, she gives one of them fishnet black stockings, another a new, longer, better, blacker dress, and still another a simple X will do, and so on. It is then that the door opens and in walks a man pushing a cart full of fresh newspapers. "Right off the flight from Dubai." He parks the cart next to the others. Only now does he say, "Good morning." But when Fatemah turns to reply, he is already at the door, his back to her, clicking the door closed. By now she has memorized the page numbers, the section, Culture, her black marker working faster. By newspaper thirty, forty, David's shorts have become less fancy, ragged at the edges. Now here's something from one of the French papers: too much cleavage showing on some blonde starlet, famous, making millions of dollars. Fatemah runs a black streak across her chest, X-ing out a hint of thigh, just in case.

By seven o'clock her fingers ache and the floor is littered with empty black markers. The same man who brought her a cart of newspapers is back, asking, "Are we finished? Should be finished. Seven o'clock, should be finished by now." But instead of waiting for an answer, he picks up one of the newspapers and thumbs through it, stopping here and there to inspect her work. He drops the paper back on the pile, and says, "Not bad." Vodka bottles that need blackening, a model's meaty thighs that require polka-dots. And so it goes.

But then one day, in the morning heat of May, Fatemah goes to work and the driver, like always, says he'll be back at seven. By now, three months into censoring, everybody knows her, waves her through security, "*As-salaam alaykum.*" And except for that one time two weeks ago, when she missed a "dangerously provocative advertisement for Southern California swimsuits," she's done her duty. In fact, the life of a censor is—how did she put it—"fun and easy and not at all what I expected." Meanwhile, back to that May morning. As she is thumbing through a London newspaper, she stops at page three. She stops and stares. She stops and stares and sits back in the chair, placing both hands in her lap. Even when he clicks open the door and wheels in his cart of newspapers, she refuses to look up, but staring down at page three, while he, like always, says, "Seven o'clock. Should be done by now. We've got to take everything to the trucks, you know. Time's up." Then, not waiting for an answer, he leaves, shutting the door behind him.

Looking down at a photograph of a blood splattered body, a child, maybe a girl, like her daughter, maybe a little boy—it is hard to tell, but blood everywhere, one leg missing, a black hole where a shoulder should be. Still on page three: photographs of starving children, all ribs and brown, slick skulls, flies walking across their faces, stopping to drink from their eyes and lips. Done staring now, having made up her mind, Fatemah picks up her black marker and makes the photos as black and nothing as she can. Blacking out, getting rid of all the death and dying. Paper after paper, page three.

Next morning, extra early for Mr. Nassir, he comes to Fatemah and tells her in his best supervisor voice that, "No. This"—holding up yesterday's London paper with black squares for photos—"is not to be censored. This is different."

Fatemah nods but it isn't the nod of understanding, because the next day, the next newspaper, there is more of the same: the Congo, a line of headless villagers on a dusty road; India, a ruined marketplace littered with blood and shoes and shattered machinery; Iraq—always Iraq—, mothers weeping over dead children. What else can she do but X it out—X all of it out.

Finally, still in May, Mr. Nassir has no choice. He tells her, "You leave me no choice." Fatemah is fired, her black markers taken away from her. But before she is escorted out of room D33, the man who wheels in the carts of newspapers waves to her like he is on holiday, saying, "Good bye." As Mr. Nassir takes Fatemah's censor's badge, he says, "News is different. People need to know what's going on. People need to see the mayhem that surrounds them." Sticking out his hand to have her shake it good-bye, he finishes with, "People need to appreciate what they have, you see, and photos like that, . . . of death and dying, make everything clear. Crystal clear."

La Vida Loca

In his room, on his bed, in a neat little row is what he will need: Rolex, cellphone, cigarettes, cigarette lighter, keys, *misbaha*, comb, wallet, sunglasses. Arms akimbo he stands there looking down at the line, the sunglasses are always problematic—although he would not use the word problematic. There is a soft knock at his door.

"*Nam?*"

"Is everything all right? Everything is there, right? What you need. It's all there?"

"Yes, Martha. Thank you."

Freshly showered, the towel around his waist, he steps to the window and pulls back the curtain to look out into the darkness, at the neighbors' wall, at the line of dusty bushes that have always been there—same size, same dust, same everything. Done looking, he pulls the curtain shut and steps away, back to the center of the room. As he does this, three things happen: he drops his towel, stares into the mirror, and sprays *Oud*. Stepping into the *Oud* is important. "Never spray *Oud* on your body—always step into it." The rest comes quickly: *dishdasha, ghutra,* and *iqal*. That part done and with Martha laughing at something funny in the kitchen, he picks up the things from the bed and loads them into his pockets. It is 9:30, time to go. Martha meets him at the door, saying, "Be careful, Nasser."

"Yes of course."

"Your mother and father have gone out, to Salmiya, to dinner, with friends."

"Good-bye, Martha."

His car is red and bright and fast, and thanks to Siera, clean. If he were to look into his mirror as he roars away, he would see Martha slanting in the doorway, waving good-bye, like a scene from one of those French films. He lights a cigarette.

Friday nights means the Arab Gulf Road, and then coffee and *shisha* with friends and later the First Ring Road. Of course traffic will be slow, but that is part of it, and from 9:30 to 10:30 he goes up and down Gulf Road, making the mandatory u-turns at Sharq and Marina Mall, revving his engine at the stoplights. Somewhere near Shaab, he pulls up next to some girl in a white BMW, sometimes staring at her with sunglasses, sometimes not—motioning for her to roll down her window, to use her cellphone, to smile back at him. But she refuses, and turns to her girlfriend and laughs. Nasser is a good boy, has always been a good boy, ask Martha, but he has never gotten used to these girls who giggle at him; and so, once the light changes, he decides to show her and her friend, and quickly angles his bright red car in front of hers, refusing to move. "How do you like that, heh?" But in his mirror he can see she is still laughing—her teeth doubly white in the darkness. There is much honking as bigger and better cars rev their engines. Some words are shouted from a yellow Hummer. Finally, he releases her and slowly drives away because although they have not stopped laughing, Nasser is certain that he has made his point. At 10:30 he is done with the Gulf Road, it is time for coffee and *shisha* and *misbaha*. His friends tell him where to meet: their place on the beach with coffee shop. Lighting another cigarette.

Nasser arrives and cannot find a place to park, but never mind, because he will wedge his car in here, behind somebody's blue Camaro. He finds Mohamad and Abdullah, and as he sits he can't help but check his watch: it is 11:00; he is behind schedule. As a result, instead of four jokes there is only time for three, and only two of the three are funny. Somebody's cousin has died in New York City—murder they think. They finger their *misbaha* and suck on their *shisha* as they consider this. Since the three of them have been friends for years, there is no need for extra talk; cellphones and *shisha* and sitting at the same table is enough, watching others watch them. The coffee shop is crowded, the sweet stink of *shisha* flooding the room. When Nasser says he must leave, Mohamad stands to say good-bye while Abdullah, on his cellphone, can only wave. Before going back to his car, he goes to the bathroom and quickly checks his pockets—yes, all is still there.

The First Ring Road is suspiciously empty, quiet. Just a butterscotch Lamborghini blaring its music. He lights a cigarette, the smoke forcing him to squint. It is then, as he comes to a red light, and still squinting, that when he glances left and right to see who is sharing the stop with him, he sees her staring at him. Her car is black with a long, angry scratch on the door, and she is staring at him. Nasser smiles and motions for her to roll down her window, but all she knows is staring. He wants her to smile, to gesture, to almost anything except this staring. He turns the mirror to look at his face, but finds nothing wrong. Finally, all he can do is look away, at the floorboard, into the neony dashboard lights. When time is up, he chances another glance her way. Her eyes haven't left him. There is no smile, no hint of recognition, just a wide-eyed stare as if she can't believe it. *Who are you?* He is glad when the light changes and he pulls away; he has no desire to seek her out in the rearview mirror. Lighting another cigarette helps.

When he returns home, only the porch light is on. Even before he has time to use his key, the door opens and Martha is there. "Everyone is asleep," she says. "Mother, father, sister, brother, it is just you and me."

"Good night, Martha," and he walks to his room, unloads his pockets and slips into bed. By now the image of the staring girl has started to fade and he can smile. Before he sleeps, he thinks of making a change, and yes, next Friday he will leave earlier, say, 9:00. For reasons he will never be sure about, Nasser dreams about the angry scratch on her car door.

The Brothers

"What's that?"

"What?"

"That?"

"What?"

"You don't hear that?"

"That?"

And so on.

Meanwhile, not far away in the double-black doorway shadows, stand two medium-sized *jinns,* one unshaven and much older than the other. The younger one leans over and whispers, "Now what do we do?"

The older one, who is picking his teeth with a fish bone, sighs, "Wait."

The younger nods as if of course he knew that. The night is starless, the trees and bushes and buildings looming gray and haggard. Over there, like a small sunrise, is the blush of the city. The younger crosses and re-crosses his arms before asking, "How'd you do that?"

"What?"

"That hissing like a snake. How'd you do that?"

The older *jinn,* who goes by the name of Omar, or sometimes Umar, once Mar, smirks, saying, "Practice. Years of practice."

"You'll teach me?"

"Of course, that's why you're here."

"When will . . ."

"Shhh, listen. You hear that?"

"What?

"Snakes. Hear that?"

The brothers stop and wait but there is only somebody's far-away laughter, followed by a barking, growling.

"Hamed, come on, we're late," he whispers, pulling at his brother's arm. *"Mom warned us about staying out late, and now we'll get it, and it's your fault because you wanted to play one more game. Your fault, not mine, now look what you've done."*

"Shut up."

"How long do we wait?" says the younger *jinn,* who has one name, Moosa, but everyone calls him Moo. "Can't we just jump out, make faces, grab their arms, maybe yank their legs?"

"It doesn't work that way. It . . . OK, there they go." Again Omar screws up his lips, sets his chin on his chest and makes a long hissing sound.

"Hamed, I'm scared. Let's run."

"No, don't you know anything? If you run they'll run. They want you to run. Just like wild dogs, you run they run and before you know it it's too late." And although the two boys don't run, they move faster, holding hands, the younger whispering, "God protect me, *Azoub be allah men ahetan al rajeem.*"

Meanwhile they stay in the shadows, the two *jinns,* their eyes burning bright, a smoldering if they stare long and hard enough.

As Moo begins to follow, Omar grabs him by the arm. "What are you doing?"

"They're getting away."

The older *jinn* throws the fish bone away and turns to take a good long look at Moo. His eyes are too far apart, his forehead a wide paperwhite. Moo has nothing like a neck. "You really don't know anything, do you?"

"I know a lot."

"What? What do you know?"

"A lot."

And so on.

Moo looks down and shuffles his feet back and forth in the dust.

Omar can only watch for so long before saying, "Take my hand."

"What?"

"My hand, take it."

When he does, the next thing he knows they are now in front of the brothers, still in the shadows but watching the brothers come toward them.

"How'd we do that?"

"Be quiet."

"Yes, but how?"

When Omar sometimes Umar said he would take Moo along to show him how it's done, he didn't really mean it; it was just one of those things you say to see how it sounds and usually it sounds pretty good, all the while expecting the other person to say, 'Thanks but no thanks.' But of course Moo is different, saying, "Let's go, I'm ready." What's a *jinn* like Omar to do but sigh and say, "Be ready at sunset."

As the two brothers scurry toward them, Moo cannot help but smile, two neat lines of shiny milkwhite teeth; this is what he's been waiting for, what he's read about, heard told around the dinner table. Omar rubs his hands together; he knows this could be special—these two brothers late for dinner. It is then that it happens: a ringing. All four stop and stare. A ringing that is full of bells. Ringing.

The brothers, all done stopping and waiting, no longer caring about holding hands, turn toward the glow of the city and run, zigzagging as they go. "*Azoub be allah men shetan al rajeem.*"

Omar waits until the brothers are out of sight, before slowly turning to face Moo.

Moo is busying "Aloing" into his cellphone.

"What are you doing?"

"Alo."

"What are you doing?"

"*Nam*, we are here," says Moo into his cellphone. "Yes, yes, of course he is with me."

Omar runs a hand over his unshaven chin, glancing one last time in the direction of the brothers. The cellphone glow stretches across Moo's face.

"So soon?" Moo's too-far-apart eyes coming together to frown. "OK, OK, *nam*, bye." And the white cellphone glare blinks off.

"I cannot believe you," hisses Omar. "Cannot."

Now it is Moo's turn to sigh. "It's Mum. We're late for dinner."

The Holy Roman Empire on a Sunday Morning

The air is brown with dust, not even brown, more like a dirty vanilla. In her car, at the gate, she waits her turn, until they are done with the car in front of her—Ms. Hunt, 10th grade history, notorious for her stories of divorce and unfriendly mothers-in-law.

His nametag says he is Khaled, and she calls him Khaled, and he smiles. "Morning Madam." Khaled has a pole and at the end of the pole is a mirror the size of two babies' heads. Khaled's job is to walk around the cars that stop at the gate with his pole with mirror to see if there are any bombs stuck to the underside of the cars. Not that Ms. Hunt would purposely place a bomb under her car—think of the dust and grime and broken fingernails. Besides, why bother with something like an engine when her purse could easily fit five maybe six sticks of dynamite. But somebody else might, at night when she is asleep, without her knowing it. Ms. Hunt parks her car outside, in the sun and dust, under the starry nights of Kuwait. Her apartment complex has nothing like real parking; wherever there is a gap between trees, any dusty space between slabs of cement will do fine. Placing a bomb under her car in the middle of the night, somewhere in the greasy glisten of the engine, in the rims of tires, would be a noisy operation, and most certainly apartment lights would come alive, curtains pulled back.

But it doesn't matter because they still need Khaled with his two-headed mirror, because you never know. You never know.

As Khaled walks around her car with his pole, he is busy looking over and talking to what has to be his supervisor, whose nametag says Johnny, who is the only one with a green uniform. Done with his walkaround, Khaled pushes a button that changes the red stoplight to green, and the hydraulic barrier hisses down, and only now is Ms. Hunt—bombless—allowed to drive into the school.

In the teacher's lounge they make the old jokes about quiet weekends, ventures to Dubai, the moveable feast called malling. Mr. Williams, Honors English, is good for at least one moveable feast joke a week. The school is like any other only dustier, hotter. There are ceiling fans that have never ever been switched off.

Except for the students, almost nobody calls her Ms. Hunt. It is Alice this, or Alice that. And this is fine; being philosophical about it, she has always been an Alice before a Ms. Hunt. When the first bell rings, she no longer hurries off to class; as a rule, students don't like it when she is in the classroom waiting for them. Better to come late, let them wait at the locked door. Mr. Wells, the Principal, recommends it. Faisal from Jabriya is the first to say good morning. Faisal is failing, has yet to turn in anything like an assignment, project, paper. His hobby, he happily admits, is smoking *shisha*. Alice secretly likes Faisal because he can still say good morning in the face of certain failure.

Like always some of them have forgotten their books, pencils. "Paper?" She nods when she hears this. In the beginning, she did not nod, nothing at all like nodding, but that was three years ago.

"Ms. Hunt, I have to go to the restroom," says Maryam.

Alice replies, "Yes, I know."

She has asked them to take care of things like bathroom and phone calls before class, and they always nod like they are hearing wisdom.

They have arrived at that part of World History where the Holy Roman Empire requires their full attention. She uses a PowerPoint that she used in graduate school, complete with timeline full of pictures of Roman aqueducts, busts of Caesar, the Coliseum. With PowerPoint loaded and ready, and with Faisal moving to the front to "get a better look," she talks about the Holy Roman Empire, what it meant to be a Roman citizen in the Empire, the pride involved in belonging to an Empire with such culture, wealth and intellect. Her PowerPoint has music, and somebody in the back asks if it is Roman music. Alice insists that it is. When she comes to somebody's illustration of a gladiator, Faisal says something. She doesn't hear but the others do and agree with him.

"What's that, Faisal? What did you say?"

He motions to the gladiator, saying, "I saw this part. The gladiator. The movie. I saw this part."

Half-way through the PowerPoint she is taken back to her graduate school days and needs both hands to help her talk, to explain the essence of Romanness. How we have learned so much from their legacy. How their history is our history, their destiny our destiny. It is interwoven, "You see? It has nothing to do with race or politics or even economics. It has nothing to do with religion. You see? It is bigger than all of that." Clasping her hands together. "Interwoven." She now must stop to ask Mohammad to stop text-messaging, and he looks up from his lap, saying, "I don't know what you're talking about."

She says, "I know."

By now Maryam has returned, sitting at her desk with folded hands. The period almost over now, her PowerPoint ending with a drawing of the twins Romulus and Remus, the founders of Rome, she cannot help but be drawn to Faisal who has watched intently, arms folded, chair tilted. She thinks he would have made a good Roman, a kind of elegance in the face of certain defeat.

By the end of the day, when she has taught her way through four periods, the Holy Roman Empire having rightfully assumed its thirty minutes of First Period, she is back in the faculty lounge. When she goes to the refrigerator to retrieve her bottle of orange juice, it is gone.

Nobody stops Alice Hunt history teacher at the gate as she leaves. There is no Khaled with his mirrored pole to look under her car, to open the hood to look into her engine. There are no red lights and barriers to keep her in. Nobody would think of sneaking bombs out of a school into the neighborhood, it just doesn't work that way.

Mr. Shehab Is Coming

"He's coming."

"Who?"

"Mr. Shehab."

"The owner?"

"Yes."

"What do we do?"

"Wash your hands."

"What?"

"Your hands and fingernails. He'll want to see your fingernails."

Mr. Shehab had spent three years at Florida State University where he learned all there is to know about fast food restaurants. "FSU, that's where I learned this business, you know." Holding his arms out wide to show us this business. "After three years, I could see what had to be done, and how to do it. Three years, no more, *sah?*" All of us neatly lined up behind the counter, aproned, capped, and nodding.

When he comes—sometimes through the back door, but more times than not through the front, tossing his *ghutra* as he enters—he only wants to see our fingernails. "That's all I need to see. That tells me all I need to know, *sah*."

Nobody knows Mr. Shehab's first name. We could guess, but even guessing never sounds right. If that weren't enough, Mr. Shehab has the whitest *dishdasha* I've ever seen, and if you happen to see him midday, in the sun, in full stride, you have to squint to look at him.

One of the first things he wants us to say to customers is "Good morning," even when it isn't. Of course only the Americans, who don't know any better, answer, Hi or Morning. The rest say nothing, or maybe grunt and then go straight to a table and smoke a cigarette and order something we don't have—have never had; they don't like it when we tell them the smoking section is not here but over there, motioning to the back tables. Sometimes when it is the middle of the day and we are especially slow, we don't mind chatting, and almost always they'll ask us if we are from Manila. Sometimes not even a question, "You're from Manila." None of us is from Manila but we say yes anyway. We are from little villages in the bluegreen hills of Cebu or Leyte that nobody has ever heard of and will never hear of unless there's a typhoon or mudslide, or some volcano erupts down the street, and then the news will be flashed around the world. But if asked, we say Manila. Mr. Shehab says it's easier that way. "Yes sir." If we still aren't busy and they're willing to listen, we might tell them our stories of family back home, the weekly phone calls to children who are with Grandma, or maybe Aunties. How every Friday at 12:00 we learn all about their spelling tests, their new reading book, about math homework gone all wrong; how Rosie called her a dirty name and that's unfair, or how Salvador earned two gold stars, and that's unfair too. In the end, our twenty minutes up, they always ask when we are coming home. How many days? *Oh, by the way, have you seen a camel yet? Ridden a camel? They bite, don't they? Rosie says they spit and bite*. Everybody agrees that this is no way to live, Western Unioning them our salary every month, seeing our children once every two years. Still, somebody has to do it.

"Are you ready for Mr. Shehab?"

"Yes."

"Show me your fingernails."

"Here."

"Yes, he will be here at any moment. Straighten your apron."

Mr. Shehab has seen to it that we have schedules. "Organization and cleanliness, those are the keys. You have these two things, everything else will fall into place, *sah*." And so every morning I clean the same windows, wipe bright the same ashtrays and salt and pepper shakers, make sure there is enough sugar, mop the same linoleum floor with the same mop that is more pole than mop. We think nothing of tips. But they don't know that; they think it will make a difference if they leave 250 *fils* on the tabletop. Only the Americans worry about what we will think of them once they are gone.

Once Mr. Shehab showed us how to say good morning, how to sweep and clean and scrub the right way, he said, "Oh, I almost forgot," placing his hand to his cheek. "Make sure you ask them how the food is: Would they like more coffee? How about water? Anything I can do for you, anything at all?" Giving his *ghutra* a flick, he ended with, "As they walk out the door, call out, 'Thank you, come again.' *Sah?*"

Mr. Shehab finally comes, and we all recite "Good morning," and he says good morning back even though he isn't American. After that, he walks straight up to Jasper and asks to see his hands. Everybody turns to watch. Jasper's job is to cook, to make jokes and to smoke two cigarettes during his breaks. It is always dangerous to ask Jasper anything because sometimes he doesn't care. Besides, he is young, without children. Today, we are lucky because he cares, and his fingernails are clean. Mr. Shehab leaves happy, and Jasper celebrates with three cigarettes during his break.

Mr. Shehab said that someday he might put a suggestion box "in the back room, next to the fire extinguisher." If he does, I might just ask him if he could spend a little less time on clean fingernails and saying Good morning and filling up coffee cups, and a little more time on finding ways so I can see my children more than once every two years. Of course it's best to write it as a question, using my best handwriting, making sure not to sign my name.

The Driver

No handshakes, no "Hellos," no "How are you, thanks for coming"—nothing like that. His first words to me were, "You see these children?" motioning to a small boy and a smaller girl behind him. "See these two?" I said I did. "Your job is very simple. Hear me? Simple." I nodded yes. "Your simple job is to get them to school on time. I don't care how you do it, just as long as it is on time and safe. Hear me? Safe," pointing his long finger in the air as if safe were up. Meanwhile, the small boy and smaller girl, having lost interest, had turned to argue over a toy truck.

Of course I said, "Yes sir."

Only then did he hold out his hand to me and I shook it, and he, smiling, said I would work out just fine. "Oh, by the way," still shaking my hand, "I'll need your passport for safe keeping." And just like that, his other non-shaking hand neatly slipped my passport into his pocket. Done shaking hands with me, done taking my passport for safe keeping, he gave me a cellphone and told me to keep it with me at all times. "If we need you we'll call. Understand?" I said I did.

As driver, the things Mr. Mohammad forgot to mention included washing cars, waxing cars, waiting, changing the oil in cars, carrying boxes and bags in and out of cars, waiting, going to MacDonald's at two o'clock in the morning to pick up the food, and maybe going back again because there were no pickles on the cheeseburgers, no salt on the fries, the chocolate milkshake "tasted funny," and so on.

The little boy, Abdulaziz, is a spy for his father; I know this, and he knows that I know this. So when he puts down his cellphone and watches, listens, I must be careful about driving too fast, weaving in and out of traffic, although school begins in five minutes. Abdulaziz cares little for what I do or say as long as he has his cellphone; he is more concerned about football, computer games, and his friends than about any driver. On Saturdays I drive from house to house to house collecting his friends: a line of three or four little boys in the back seat, staring long and hard into their cellphones, calling other people, playing cellphone games, not saying a word to one another. When they do talk, they all agree that school is always getting in the way of more important things. But when Abdulaziz puts down his cellphone and I catch him staring at me in the mirror, I must be careful and slow down, use my turn signals, be sure to laugh if he decides to tell me a joke.

The smaller one, Sarah, cares nothing for me. In fact, after all this time, I am certain that she doesn't even know my name. To her I am the driver, or him. Come to think of it, she isn't wrong: at nine years old what use are drivers' names when there are cartoons to watch, dolls to play with, pretty pink shoes to wear?

When I pick them up from school, double parked, sometimes triple parked, of course there is always the honking, bits and pieces of shouting, but even I can tell it's a fake anger, impatience, and their hearts aren't in it. Besides, I have learned to raise my hand—something like a wave—that says: "I'm sorry, I know. My mistake, I won't be long," and so on. A simple raised hand makes everything all right. As driver, much of my job is waiting, and when I do I sometimes chat with the other drivers. We stand in small circles and trade bits of news, rumor, gossip. By now we know each other by first name, by what village we are from; some of us know the same people back in India. Andrew, two streets over, and I even have the same second cousin. As we talk we can't help but glance at our cellphones—just in case.

The days Abdulaziz decides to wear his father's sunglasses can make things doubly difficult. On those days, he can't understand why I don't park closer to the school, to the main gate. "Everybody else does it." On the days of his father's sunglasses he will insist that I turn off the engine and open the door for him, that I carry his bag to the classroom and hold his homework "like this," or "Walk behind me, two steps." When we get to the classroom, he says I must place his bag, "Here, . . . no, there." If girls are watching, he'll say, "Now you can go."

I live in a room between the dog pen and the street. I have a bed and a toilet. I have my own television. The cellphone he gave me that first day is the most expensive thing I own.

Although I have been with the Mohammads for five years, I don't love these children and their family. They are just people who I ferry here and there. I have my own family to love, two small daughters who simply know me as the man who calls every Wednesday at 8:00, who visits them once every two years, who they are anxious to see because Mommy says so, who they know as Papa because I bring them presents and candies. Although Mr. Mohammad and his family like things that are big—big cars, big televisions, long, wide carpets, large, loud German Shepherds, a house the size of a small hotel—they would never be happy in a large country like mine. They would be unhappy in my village, my house; their unhappiness would be the same as mine but different. My sadness has nothing to do with size or sunglasses or cellphones.

The Maid

They joke about how every Christmastime I go bad. That's what Abdulaziz, the oldest, says, "Auntie's going bad again." And he's not wrong because for the last six winters it's happened like clockwork. One morning I simply can't pull myself out of bed to do it; it's as if overnight I've become full to overflowing with everything: slipping out of bed at sunrise, making their lunches and then walking upstairs, checking to see if their eyes are open and no they aren't and so shaking them awake, and having them groan, "Go away," but never mind that, asking them what they need ironed, brushed, polished, followed by, "Let me sleep," and then going back down the stairs to cook their breakfasts and then answer the telephone and feed the cat because it's always hungry, and back up the stairs to see if they really are out of bed and moving towards the bathroom and getting dressed and, finally, hearing them shuffle towards the table to eat, and now, the cat still worming around my feet, asking for yet more food, but I must hurry to answer the telephone again because everybody's too tired to walk that far, and. . . . All the while Mr. Mohammad and Madam are asleep in their bed, in their bedroom, the door tightly shut.

Mr. Mohammad insists it's a trick to get more money, a bigger salary, more vacation time; and of course, that's the joking part of him, and yet, over the years, I've learned about that other, bigger part of him that's not joking and unfriendly and probably some other words that I'm not sure about. But I never think about it like money. All I know is that when it arrives it covers me like one of those sudden afternoon sandstorms, and I can't see or breathe. I can't move. I close my door, pull the curtain shut and take to bed. I have no strength to leave my room. I think of my real family, my daughters who live in our village, on the edge of a wet bluegreen forest, who every year beg me to come home, saying, enough is enough, and, "We'll find a way to pay the rent, the bills, but come home because we miss you terribly. Christmas is not the same without you." My son, who's almost Mr. Mohammad's age, who during the day works on a farm, cutting sugarcane and herding cows, and during the night, to make extra money, does something else that nobody wants to talk about. All of them saying it's Christmastime and, "For goodness sakes it's time to come home." I pull the sheet over my head to make everything doubly dark.

In the afternoon, when they return from school and don't find me at the front door waiting for them, holding out my hands to take their backpacks, to listen to their stories of mean teachers and unfriendly friends, suddenly they will remember I have gone bad and hurry to my room and gently click open the door, trying to be quiet but not really, whispering and giggling and whispering until finally, in the half-light, they find the edge of the bed and gather around to pat my hand, stroke my arm, pet my hair, whispering that they need me, can't live without me. I try to pull the sheet over my head but they won't let me. The little ones' tears are real because they are too young to know any better. Abdulaziz will come in later, once the others have left, and stand next to the bed; I will pretend to be asleep, and he will say nothing, only watch, as if the watching tells him all he needs to know. Done watching, he goes to his room, leaving my door wide open.

By day two, I will sniff and feel a little better, and Mr. Mohammad will come in and promise to raise my wages, or "How about more vacation time?" Sometimes the extra vacation time happens, but never more wages. All the while Madam says nothing. She refuses to even visit my room. She knows there is nothing to say, nothing to do. She knows. By the cool of January, I have completely recovered and with Christmas come and gone and my real family grown quiet for the time being, we pretend that nothing has happened and everything slips back to the way it was.

In the beginning, I learned very quickly to answer to Nanny, Auntie, Maid, Miss Sally, even Domestic Help but this last one is something from the newspapers, and Mr. Mohammad says it as a joke. That was before Thomas, the gardener, when Mr. Mohammad had me watering the lawn, raking a garden that was more sand than grass and flowers and leaves. That was before he gave me Friday mornings off. "Sleep in. Watch your TV programs. Relax. The morning is all yours."

When every other August comes around and it is time for me to visit my real family, Mr. Mohammad likes to play a game of not giving me my passport, of saying he's lost it, misplaced it, or, "You really don't need a vacation, do you? Your family is here with us." It's a good joke and I play along until he mysteriously finds my passport and gives it to me laughing. Again, these are the two parts of Mr. Mohammad: the fun, playful part and the bigger darker part that enjoys seeing me worry. I secretly think he can't believe that after six years his family is not my family too. After all, he does pay my salary.

The Gardener

Mr. Mohammad's garden is not. It starts off with a line of yellow-brown bushes followed by a patch of lawn that is more patch than lawn, and after that a cluster of flowers near the front door, and then somebody's too-fat cat that comes out to watch me water, the hose twitching and shivering as I go from flower to flower to flower.

That first day five years ago, Mr. Mohammad shook my hand, and then handed me a long list of things a gardener needs to do, needs to know. Actually that is not entirely true, it was the other way around, first he handed me the long list then asked me to read it and I did and after I finished he asked if I had any questions, and I said just one, "Where do you keep the hose?" Then he shook my hand, saying, "I like your attitude." I didn't tell him that his list was for children, not gardeners.

Sometimes in the early evening, the sun still a red idea beyond the sand and dust, Mr. Mohammad will step out into the garden and with cigarette in hand we will debate what is a weed and what is not, what green growing out of the sand is the stuff of garden. Our debates are short and full of What do you means and Believe me I know what I'm talking abouts, and I always let him win. In the end, I often water the weeds that he insists are special Arab flowers, "treasures of the desert." Although I have never been good at numbers, I can say that from here to there, Mr. Al-Shatti's fence, twenty-five percent of Mr. Mohammad's garden is healthy weeds. As we walk and talk he will smoke two maybe three cigarettes, flicking each finished cigarette over his shoulder into the garden. Once he is done debating and steps back into his house, I water the lawn and the row of flowers; I stop the cats from digging their holes, wrestling flower stems to the ground. I retrace our walk and pick up his cigarette butts. Mr. Mohammad is not interested in what I can do, just what I need to do. He is interested in winning our short debates. And that's all right because Mr. Mohammad pays my wages—he has my passport. I will water all the weeds he wants me to.

When I first arrived, that first day after the list and handshake, I went to my room and took out a piece of paper and pencil and designed a proper garden. One with three rows of green vegetables, a vast square of lush green grass, three palms there, four over there, a spiral of purple and white flowers flowing from one end of the garden and back again. That was in the beginning.

Fridays are the best days for gardening because Mr. Mohammad is too busy to be bothered with me and his garden. Although the somebody's too-fat black cat is always there, crouching in the weeds, ears back, tail twitching, ready to pounce on the hose that quivers every time I water, on Fridays I take a chance and pull some of the weeds he insists are flowers, stuffing them into a black garbage bag. I have taken even a bigger chance and purchased some seeds that guarantee red and white flowers. In fact, the packet reads: "wondrous red and white flowers." I have planted them at the very edge of the garden, near Mr. Al-Shatti's fence. Mr. Mohammad almost never walks that far into his garden. Mr. Mohammad does not like Mr. Al-Shatti for many reasons: he has too much of the wrong *wasta,* he always leaves the country during Ramadan. Mr. Al-Shatti's children are too loud. But most importantly, Mr. Al-Shatti's garden is bigger and greener, his garden has a pond with a tiny waterfall. He has lights that twinkle in the trees.

The children, Abdulaziz and the girls, don't come to the garden unless she is angry with them and wants them out of the house. "Get out. Go play. Go to the garden." They see the garden as a punishment, something like an exile, and since there is no shade, no palms or trees, in the middle of the day, they are right. Abdulaziz is famous for his pouting, and when he is sent to the garden he is quick to trample flowers, kick sand into the grass, say things to me in Arabic that he thinks I don't understand. The girls are different; they are too young to sulk for very long. They ignore me. Sometimes they turn on the hose and squirt each other, and the cat. Other times they play games that have to do with taking big steps and numbers. In the end, it isn't long before she will come to the door and shout, "What are you doing there in the heat? Put that hose down and get inside right this minute," slamming the door to show them what a "this minute" sounds like. Meanwhile, Abdulaziz is nowhere to be seen because he has slipped back into the house long ago.

Next to my room is the garden room. That's what Mr. Mohammad calls it—the garden room. I call it the room next to my room. Sometimes when he walks in the garden with his friends and visitors, he will be sure to stop and point, saying, "And that's the garden room." Visitors nod like it's a good idea. In the garden room there is a shovel, a rake, a hoe, and the hose that the too-fat cat can't believe is not some kind of long green snake. There are two baskets, one inside the other. In the garden room are three empty shelves. Of course, Mr. Mohammad does not need a gardener, will never need a gardener, but Mr. Al-Shatti and Mr. Mohammad's brother in Misref have gardeners. Still showing visitors the garden, if Mr. Mohammad happens to see me, he will be sure to introduce me as "My gardener."

The Conference on Rights and Freedom

"Say that one more time."

"Which part?"

"The last part. Say that last part again."

Almost as if rehearsed, the two of them sigh as one, and then Maryam with the fire-engine red lipstick, with the too much mascara that makes her look weary and bruised, begins. "It's all very simple: at the end of our presentation, Sara and I will stand up and remove our *hijabs*."

I nod and wait to see if there is more, something I might have missed. From somewhere in the hallway, somebody's cellphone plays Beethoven's Fifth. A door opens and closes, and then opens again. Finally, the waiting all used up, I say, "And tell me again why you think this is a good idea?"

She has not stopped bouncing her right leg since she sat down, as if it has its own private motor that has nothing to do with the rest of her. The other, Sara, smiles; when she turns to look at the bookcase she smiles; as she tilts her head to read the titles she smiles; she smiles at the window. Once she has spread her smile to all parts of my office, she returns to me, smiling.

"Our presentation has been accepted by the Denver, Colorado conference, and we have something to say, something to show. We are not afraid if that's what you're thinking, not at all."

"No. I wasn't thinking fear, but something else, something . . ."

"What?"

"I think it's this: why turn something as serious, as important as this into a sideshow? A circus? Is that what you're all about?"

Another piece of collective sighing, followed by, "No of course not, we want to show them who we are, not who they think we are according to TV and the movies. Why can't we do that? What's wrong with that? They think this," fingering her *hijab,* "this equals oppression; they think being veiled is a weakness; they believe we don't have choices, freedoms, rights. They know nothing, they don't know us, and for thirty minutes on a Saturday morning in Denver, Colorado, we will show them. We'll show them all. We want to make a statement. Those people, those westerners," making tiny circles with her hands to show me what westerners look like, "don't know anything about us, just what they read, what the news shows them, tells them."

A student appears at the doorway, signaling that he needs to come in, and I wave him away.

When the two of them first walked in I could see they thought about shutting the door behind them, but then, as one, changed their mind. They slipped neatly into the chairs, arms folded.

"Why?"

"Sorry, what did you say?"

"Why should you care what they think? What anybody thinks?"

"It's important. It has to be."

Suddenly Maryam does two things: she stops bouncing her leg and reaches up to tuck a wisp of hair back under her *hijab.*

"Why did you say that?"

"What?"

"That."

Sara's smile dims.

"You don't think it has anything to do with them, with others, do you? You think it's us, don't you? You think it's all an excuse."

When I say, "I am not against this," they look at one another, and Maryam, leg restarted, says, "We aren't looking for your approval. That's the problem, that's always been the problem. What we can and can't do, what we can and can't wear, see, say. We're just telling you this is our plan for Denver, Colorado."

I reach over and pick up a pencil from the corner of my desk. I almost never use pencils, and I am not even sure how this one got there, but there it is and I pick it up and study its pink eraser. I turn it once, twice; my studying all done, I say, "Once upon a time you decided to cover, to wear the *hijab*. Right?"

"This is true, at fifteen I thought it was a good idea. My mother thought it was a good idea. My father and grandfather and uncles and aunts, all of them thought it was a good idea. And, in the end, so did I. But now, 6 years later, . . . I've changed, you see. Both of us have."

"You have a duty to your faith, do you not?"

"Our faith."

When another student walks by once, twice and even a third time, I come out from behind my desk and click the door shut.

"And ourselves? How about us?" fingertips tapping her shoulder.

All the while Sara, who has been watching us like at a tennis match, smiling one way, then the other, clears her throat, pulls at the edges of her *hijab*, and says, "Isn't it OK to change? To change our mind? Why is it against the rules? People change. Isn't that the way of the world? You think we don't know what this means, what did you call it, this unveiling? You don't think we understand the implications? Of course we do. But we can't be afraid. Fear is not our friend, even I know that."

Both of us stare at her.

"We are not all bombs and beards and *burqas*."

I put the pencil down.

"Did you read that somewhere?"

"Yes, but so what. It's still true. We are not crazy people."

Now it is my turn to sigh. "But this is bigger than just you, the two of you. It's about a belief, a concept. It's about obligation."

"And how about us? The two of us?"

"Some people will not like this, this unveiling of yours in public, in front of strangers."

She picks up the yellow pencil, clutching it in her fist, saying, "It does not matter. Some will dislike us simply because we wear the *hijab,* knowing nothing about us but what we wear. So what does it matter? There are haters everywhere, for no good reason. I can't worry about them. I won't be held hostage to other people's fears."

Others shuffle in the hallway, and someone, somewhere, laughs loud and long. My telephone rings, and I can tell they like it when I let it ring, not answering. Finally, after assorted frowns and whispers, they reach a decision, and Maryam lifts a piece of paper from her purse. "We want to show you something." Now I can see that it is more than a piece of paper, it's a blackandwhite photograph. She slides it across the desktop. Of course it is the two of them, unveiled, side by side, long hair flowing, swirling around their throats and shoulders.

I stare at the photo.

As they wait, sighing, smiling, leg bouncing, I pick it up to look closer, harder. It is then, like an electric shock, that all is made clear. The photo is evidence of their double lives. Young faces with dark cascading hair, a new brightness in their eyes, an image that has nothing to do with *hijabs*. In the photo I can see their dimples. I stare because they are right, but even as I think it I don't know what I mean. All this talk of right and wrong, good and bad disappears into the blackandwhite photo of two young women. This is the flesh and bone and blood of it. They are right: there is a difference. There is an otherness that is bigger, beyond the stuff of religion, but I don't know what to call it. I don't dare call it freedom. But yes, there it is—in blackandwhite.

Following My Green Shirt

That's my green shirt walking down the street. At first I wasn't sure, glancing once, twice, after all, there are a lot of green shirts in the world. But then as he slows to get a good hard look at something in the gutter, I walk faster, catching up to him, and there it is: a thin bleach stain running down the right shoulder, a watery non-green at the elbows, the frayed collar: my green shirt. Once he finishes with the gutter—somebody's stiff-legged dead calico—nudging it with the toe of his sandal, he with my-once green shirt moves on. And all I can do is follow.

Three or four days ago, maybe more, as we aimed for the front door, getting ready to leave, she stopped to let me know what she had done, her good idea in the spirit of Ramadan. She had gone through my closet, coat hanger by coat hanger, deciding what I no longer needed, what no longer looked right for me. That's what she said, "The stuff that no longer looks right for someone like you." I nodded to show her I was not against good ideas. But later that night, while Girgian children were at the door singing their song, curious to see what she had taken, I quietly pulled open the closet door, running my fingers along the line of coat hangers, opening drawers. I had readied myself for some kind of anger, but nothing came of it. I turned on all the lights and looked again, harder, deeper into the closet. Aside from a neat stack of empty hangers, I couldn't tell what was missing. This was both good and bad.

I follow him, him and my green shirt, as far as the corner *bakala*, and when he enters I quickly follow. Once inside, shoulder to shoulder, I get a good look at his-now green shirt. Sadly, it fits him surprisingly well, as if it's been his all along. When he brushes by me to grab a bag of potato chips, I can smell our laundry soap, and yes, now facing me, I can see where that top button is gone, the one she promised to sew on two, three years ago.

And so she had given my clothes to charity, folding everything neatly into one of those black garbage bags, and giving it to Sarah, whose friend knows a friend who is all about charities come Ramadan. Although I am not sure about the folding part, or even placing everything neatly into a black garbage bag, I know her, and that is what she did, or something like it, on a Friday, or maybe a Saturday.

He has long fingers and square, yellow fingernails, but no rings; his wristwatch is too large, with three small dials just in case he might need to know the time in Buenos Aires, or maybe Tokyo. He and the *bakala* man joke with each other like long-time friends. Now the *bakala* man motions to our green shirt, saying something that I can't hear but I am sure it has to do with clothes, green shirts. With *Iftar* only two or three hours away, he buys cigarettes and a bag of potato chips. I don't smoke, have never even thought of it as an interesting idea, and as I watch him pay, taking money from the pocket that has always held my best pen, I secretly, silently feel a pang of sorrow. After all these years the green shirt is not used to the stink of cigarettes. Even as I think it, I laugh, and the *bakala* man looks up in surprise. I motion with my hand, saying, "It's nothing." I buy some chewing gum that I don't need, don't want, and look down at the many boxes of candy. Before he leaves, they shake hands twice. Finally, all done, he steps back into the heat, and that's when I see the sweaty beginnings of a dark line along his spine, a growing darkness under his right arm.

As he disappears around the corner, I slow, stop, wondering what this following is all about. Do I demand my green shirt back? *That's my green shirt you're wearing, you know. My shirt*. Snickering, I stuff my hands as deep into my pockets as they will go. It is then, with my-once green shirt gone, that I see coming towards me what has to be my Christmas gift of three years ago: brown trousers with torn belt-loop flapping in the breeze. The best I can do is drop to one knee to tie a shoelace that does not need tying. He is too short for my brown trousers, as they bunch at his shoes. He is on his cellphone talking, now laughing. His hair is long and I can't imagine what can be so funny. Meanwhile, my brown trousers with broken belt-loop are edging closer until, if I want to, I can reach out and touch them as they stroll by. It is then that he sees me, on one knee, and stops talking and laughing long enough to wish me a "*Ramadan Kareem*."

I don't mind her giving away old clothes to those who need them, to those who can use them. It's not a bad idea, and she isn't wrong. But it's bigger than that, it's beyond Ramadan and charity; it has to do with seeing strangers wearing your pants, your-once shirts, with seeing your sockless, dusty-black shoes cross the street. There is something all wrong with following your clothes down the street.

The Stalled Water Truck and Other Impatience

If they had decided to stop their conversation long enough to turn around and look out the coffee shop window, they would have seen one of those bulky water trucks slowing, and now edging towards the side of the road, and finally grinding to a halt; and if they had looked they would have seen cars lined up unhappily behind it, honking, flashing their lights. They would have seen the water truck driver throwing open his door, jumping out and scurrying to look at all four wheels. Of course the drivers waiting behind him care nothing for things like that, and so the honking continues. The truck driver is motioning that he can only do so much, raising both hands to beg for a little patience. "*Sabr, sabr.*" Now, done with the wheels, he climbs up to check the engine. Meanwhile, back at the coffee shop.

"Did I hear you right?"

"What?"

"That last part about him being married."

"Yes, he is married."

"Married?"

"Yes."

"And how about that other part?"

"What other part?"

"How he won't divorce?"

"They're separated, and have been for three years. They might as well be divorced."

"And he won't divorce?"

"It's complicated."

"He won't divorce, even though he loves you? He has said this to you, yes? 'I love you'? 'I want to share my life with you'? If I remember right, people in love say things like this, yes?"

"Yes. But it's complicated."

The stalled water truck driver is motioning for the cars to go around, to stop honking and gesturing and rolling down their windows to yell at him, but to go around. It is very simple. And if the two of them had stopped talking long enough to listen, to push open the coffee shop window, they would have heard him saying, "*Baseta, baseta.*" It's simple."

"And you are OK with this: him not divorcing?"

"Yes."

"In essence you will be his second wife?"

"In essence."

"His second wife."

"They have been separated for years, I tell you. She lives in Jordan, he is here. She has her own job, apartment, her parents are there. He can see the children anytime he wants, and in the summer they stay with him for two, three weeks. His two daughters are very cute. I have seen their photos. Very cute. It's all set."

"You will be his second wife?"

"Yes, but I tell you it will be like his only wife, because he doesn't talk to her except when it has something to do with the kids, and that is almost never."

"All of this he has told you?"

"Yes, and I believe him. Why shouldn't I? I have known him for years, even before he married."

"Why not insist that he divorce? If he loves you, divorce is nothing. Start off fresh and new. Give yourself a chance."

"But what if it doesn't work?"

"What?"

"What if I insist he divorce and he does because he loves me and I love him and then, after we marry, it doesn't work between us; in one or two years everything goes wrong and we separate, even divorce. I would feel terrible because I was the one who insisted he divorce in the first place. Terrible."

The stalled water truck driver is not a big man, and when he leans into the engine to see what the problem is, he looks even smaller, as if the truck, if it wanted to, could consume him in one watery truck gulp.

"You're serious? What you just said, You're serious?"

"*Tabyan*. Of course."

"If he loves you, he should divorce. If I loved someone this is what I would do, say, but maybe he's different."

"No, he has said as much. But he has the two children."

"Yes?"

"What about them?"

"They live with their mother?"

"Yes."

"Whether divorced or not, seeing children does not change, does it?"

"I don't know. I don't want to talk about it anymore. You're confusing everything."

The water truck driver has stepped away from the engine and suddenly he is carrying a bucket and moving to the rear of the truck. And if the coffee shop window had still been open, they would have heard the drivers behind him yelling, cursing. But the truck driver no longer cares because he is at the rear of the truck and there is a valve that he turns and water comes gushing out. He fills the bucket. Once it is full, he closes the valve and heads back to the engine.

"Everything was perfect until you started talking."

"Sorry."

"People like you don't understand. Second wives are nothing in this part of the world. Nothing. Your one-wife thinking is for another world, another culture. It's not the same here. Doesn't have to be the same. If you love someone, other wives mean nothing. Being a *daraya* to someone else is nothing. You see? Nothing."

Once he puts water in the truck's radiator, the bucket disappears and he gets back into the truck. He puts the water truck in gear and lurches back into traffic, almost hitting a car that is trying to get around him. One last time he sticks his hand out the window, and screams, "*Sabr, habibi, sabr.*"

"No, I don't see."